NEW YORK REVIEW BOOKS
CLASSICS

NO ROOM AT THE MORGUE

JEAN-PATRICK MANCHETTE (1942–1995) was a genre-redefining French crime novelist, screenwriter, critic, and translator. Born in Marseilles to a family of relatively modest means, Manchette grew up in a southwestern suburb of Paris, where he wrote from an early age. While a student of English literature at the Sorbonne, he contributed articles to the newspaper *La Voie communiste* and became active in the national students' union. In 1961 he married, and with his wife, Mélissa, began translating American crime fiction—he would go on to translate the works of such writers as Donald Westlake, Ross Thomas, and Margaret Millar, often for Gallimard's Série Noire. Throughout the 1960s Manchette supported himself with various jobs writing television scripts, screenplays, young-adult books, and film novelizations. In 1971 he published his first novel, a collaboration with Jean-Pierre Bastid, and embarked on his literary career in earnest, producing ten subsequent works over the course of the next two decades and establishing a new genre of French novel, the *néo-polar* (distinguished from the traditional detective novel, or *polar*, by its political engagement and social radicalism). During the 1980s, Manchette published a celebrated translation of Alan Moore's *Watchmen* graphic novel for a bande-dessinée publishing house co-founded by his son, Doug Headline. In addition to *Fatale*, *The Mad and the Bad*, *Nada*, and *Ivory Pearl* (all available from NYRB Classics), Manchette's novels *Three to Kill* and *The Prone Gunman*, as well as Jacques Tardi's graphic-novel adaptations of them (titled *West Coast Blues* and *Like a Sniper Lining Up His Shot*, respectively), are available in English.

ALYSON WATERS has translated works by Albert Cossery, Louis Aragon, René Belletto, and others. She teaches literary translation in the French department of Yale University and is the managing editor of Yale French Studies. For NYRB Classics, Waters has translated Emmanuel Bove's *Henri Duchemin and His Shadows* and Jean Giono's *A King Alone*.

HOWARD A. RODMAN is the author of the novels *Destiny Express* and *The Great Eastern* and the screenplays *Joe Gould's Secret* and *Savage Grace*. He is a past president of the Writers Guild of America West and a Chevalier de l'Ordre des Arts et des Lettres.

NO ROOM AT THE MORGUE

JEAN-PATRICK MANCHETTE

Translated from the French by
ALYSON WATERS

Afterword by
HOWARD A. RODMAN

NEW YORK REVIEW BOOKS

New York

THIS IS A NEW YORK REVIEW BOOK
PUBLISHED BY THE NEW YORK REVIEW OF BOOKS
207 East 32nd Street, New York, NY 10016
www.nyrb.com

Originally published in the French language as *Morgue pleine*.
First published as a New York Review Books Classic in 2020.

This work received support from the French Ministry of Foreign Affairs and
the Cultural Services of the French Embassy in the United States through their
publishing assistance program.

Library of Congress Cataloging-in-Publication Data
Names: Manchette, Jean-Patrick, 1942–1995 author. | Waters, Alyson, 1955–
    translator.
Title: No room at the morgue / by Jean-Patrick Manchette ; translated from the
    French by Alyson Waters.
Other titles: Morgue pleine. English
Description: New York : New York Review Books, [2020] | Series: New York
    review books classics
Identifiers: LCCN 2019058956 (print) | LCCN 2019058957 (ebook) | ISBN
    9781681374185 (paperback) | ISBN 9781681374192 (ebook)
Classification: LCC PQ2673.A452 M6713 2020 (print) | LCC PQ2673.A452
    (ebook) | DDC 843/.914—dc23
LC record available at https://lccn.loc.gov/2019058956
LC ebook record available at https://lccn.loc.gov/2019058957

ISBN 978-1-68137-418-5
Available as an electronic book; ISBN 978-1-68137-419-2

Printed in the United States of America on acid-free paper.
10 9 8 7 6 5 4 3

I

MONDAY was particularly depressing. My alarm went off at nine and I sat up in bed. Well, if you can call it a bed. Besides, I'd already been half-awake for a couple of hours. I'd gone to sleep at ten thirty the night before. I sleep a lot. Or rather, I'm half-awake a lot. It depends on when you catch me.

I made the "bed," placing the shredded blue velvet slipcover on it, raising the back and armrests, and pushing the whole lot against the wall. It almost looked like a sofa, sort of.

I was in my briefs. It was chilly. It was a rotten spring as springs go, and it'd started raining in the courtyard outside the frosted window and probably on the rest of the city too. Still, I opened the place up to air it out, and as a result water came in and dripped down the wall below. I closed the window. I put the magazines in the magazine rack, old copies of *L'Express*, *Paris Match*, *Reader's Digest*, a stray *Newsweek* from who knows where. It's not that I speak American or anything, but it all makes me look international, broadminded.

In whose eyes?

I walked through the office to get to the kitchen. I washed my face and shaved over the sink. While I was shaving, I saw my face as usual in the rectangular mirror hanging from the pipe. Of course I cut myself and it took me a while to stanch the oozing blood. By the time I left the apartment (two rooms and a kitchen), it was almost ten. I made a pit stop on the landing at the shared toilet then walked down the stairs (fifth floor, no elevator) to grab a coffee at the place on the corner of rue Saint-Martin. On the roadway, the cars were flowing smoothly. Ten years ago, it would've been called a traffic jam, but now they say it's "flowing smoothly." "Flowing," maybe, but there's still a definite smell of gas. The whores had already beaten their retreat from the sidewalk to the hotel entrances. Ten years from now, even those women won't be able to tolerate it here; they'll suffocate to death, or else they'll go hawk their wares in the countryside.

I broke my last one-hundred-franc bill to pay for my coffee. I needed to go to the bank, but how much did I have left in there anyway? Less than a grand. And everything due in a month and a half. One hundred and twenty thousand. Things weren't looking so hot for me.

I climbed back up to my place and the five flights sapped all my energy. No wonder no one comes up to see me. How long had I been here? Almost three months. Just long enough to eat through my savings. Standing in front of my door, I stared at the business card tacked on it: E. TARPON, PRIVATE INVESTIGATOR. The edges of the card were slowly but surely curling in and turning yellow. Maybe I should put a nameplate downstairs. But why bother? Today everyone telephones first. Just then, my phone rang inside.

I grabbed the keys from my pocket and went in. I crossed through the waiting room, that is, my bedroom, and picked up the phone on the desk.

"Eugène?"

"Who's calling?" I said.

"Foran. Remember me?"

"You've gotta be kidding! You in Paris?"

"Have been for three weeks. I quit too."

"Really? How come?"

"I'll tell you. Can I see you?"

"Ehhh, well…"

"Let's have lunch together. You're near Les Halles, right? There're some good joints over there. I'll come get you."

I said fine and he said he didn't have time to talk just then but that he'd tell me everything over lunch. And then he hung up, and so did I. I didn't really feel like seeing Foran.

Not much happened between the time he called and the time he arrived. I did my bodybuilding. I washed a few things in the kitchen sink and had just finished hanging them up to dry when the doorbell rang. Eleven thirty. A bit early for Foran. Maybe it was a client. I dried my hands, put my jacket back on, and went to open the door. It was the Jehovah's Witnesses. I very nicely told them to fuck off. They left me a pamphlet; I tossed it in the trash without reading it. At least now there was something in my wastebasket.

It made me look busy.

Next, I took a book from the shelves in the waiting room and sat down on the blue sofa. I could hear Stanislavski's sewing machine. He's the tailor who lives upstairs. The book was about the generation gap in a wealthy family. The kid was turning out bad and wanted to do the hippy thing. The father was fighting with all his might against this evil penchant and in the end he triumphed, but little by little he'd lost his lust for life and, when the kid finally decided to take the straight and narrow and become an executive like every-one else, it was the father who split. He disappeared completely and the author just left us hanging, which I felt was rather unfair. I would've wanted to know what came next, what happened to the father. No doubt the author couldn't think that far ahead.

Then the doorbell rang again. I set down my book and went to answer. It was Foran. He'd grown even fatter, but he was dressed as a civilian so he looked less like Hermann Goering than before. He was wearing a blue suit with a red tie over a white shirt, and his face looked like a French flag too: little blue eyes in a fat red face beneath a dirty blond crew cut. He was panting. For a moment he didn't move, unable to say a word. Then: "Your stairs are a killer. Do clients actually make it up here?"

I shrugged.

"How are you?" I asked.

"I'm okay. Gonna offer me a drink?"

I led him into the office.

"Sit down."

I walked into the kitchen and shut the door behind me. I poured out two glasses of pastis and placed them on a tray with a carafe of water and went back to the office.

"I don't have any ice," I informed him.

He didn't answer. He didn't sit. He was walking around the room, examining everything: the ersatz oak desk with drawers on both sides, the metal filing cabinet, which was empty, the plywood chair, and the imitation leather armchair. A Martini ashtray and a lamp on the desk. The Jehovah's Witness pamphlet in the wastebasket. Cigarette burns on the carpet.

"How's business?" he asked.

"Can't you see?"

"Not so good, huh?"

I shrugged again. He poured some water in our glasses and clinked his against mine, which was still on the desk.

"That's exactly why I wanted to see you. I have a job for you. You're not overworked, far as I can tell?"

"What kind of job?"

"We'll talk about it over lunch."

The last thing I wanted was to have lunch with Foran.

"What kind of job?" I said again.

He sat down in the armchair, swirled the pastis in his glass, and smiled at me.

"Still bitter, eh? Still suspicious? Once bitten, eh? Get off your cloud, Eugène. You're not doing a thing here, and we both know it. Maybe one or two little jobs since you set up shop. A divorce. An accountant to keep an eye on. And that's putting everything in the best light. Right?"

I sat down on the chair and sipped my warm pastis.

"You're such a bore, Foran. Tell me what you have in mind, and then maybe we'll get lunch. But we'll go Dutch. That's how things stand between us."

He kept smiling a little longer, and then his smile jumped ship.

"Fine, fine," he said. "If that's how it is. I'm getting a team together. Gumshoes too, but I work in the real world, not in the dream world. I got my contacts ahead of time with the big companies. The job is to train and supervise security guards. But we'll need to be five or six guys. I thought of you."

"Supervise security guards," I repeated. "And what would they be guarding?"

"Factory security guards."

"I see."

"The time is right," he said and his smile came back on board.

"I see," I repeated. "Fuck off."

He thought he'd misheard me.

"Out," I said. "Disappear. Go screw yourself."

He didn't even get angry. He stood up shaking his head, and his pudgy lips formed an amused little pout.

"Silly of you to be so stubborn," he said. "But I get it. I won't hold it against you. I'll leave you my card."

"Don't bother."

"You might change your mind. It's happened."

"Farewell, Foran," I said.

He took the time to empty his glass, then gave me an ironic little wave with his fat little hand. And he left. I picked up the card he'd placed on the edge of my desk. It was printed in brown on stock the color of rancid butter, looking nothing like a normal calling card—more like a restaurant owner's business card. It said: INDUSTRIAL SUPPORT AND SECURITY, below that: CHARLES FORAN, DIRECTOR, below that: BY FORMER MEMBERS OF THE NATIONAL GENDARMERIE AND ARMED FORCES. *OUR EMPLOYEES ARE EXCLUSIVELY FRENCH*, and finally an address in Saint-Cloud and a phone number. On the back, in ornate letters, *ISS* was inscribed.

I twirled the card in my fingers for a moment, then let out a deep sigh and tore it up. I threw the pieces in the wastebasket, next to the religious pamphlet. I was looking busier and busier. At that rate, after six months to a year, my wastebasket stood a good chance of being full.

There were two eggs and some cheese left in the fridge. I ate it all for lunch. I didn't feel like going downstairs to buy anything else. I washed the frying pan, the plate, the knife and fork, and my glass along with Foran's. I made myself an instant coffee and carried it into the vestibule. The flowers in the vase on the pedestal table were dead. I went to throw them out and came back to sit on the blue sofa. I stayed there for a long time without doing anything at all, then I read a few pages of a book that Stanislavski had lent me: *The New Society*, by someone named Merlino. It's from 1893 and rather badly printed. I couldn't manage to get into it. Everything Stanislavski lends me is really strange.

Finally I went back into my office and picked up the phone. It took a few moments to be connected to the number I requested in the Allier region.

"Hello?" I heard in the distance.

"You're through, caller!" shouted the operator in an urgent voice.

"Hello," I said. "Is this the Chartier Hotel?"

A series of loud noises followed. I heard someone impatiently shout "Hello? Hello?" Then all of a sudden the line was clear and a voice practically burst my eardrum.

"Who's calling?"

"Eugène Tarpon. Is this Madame Marthe?"

It was. She wanted to know how I was doing, and I said fine and could she go get my mother? She said okay and I could tell she wasn't happy because I didn't bother to ask for news about the village, who had died recently, and all those other cheerful things.

It took my mother a while to come to the phone. She lives fifty meters from the Chartier Hotel but she's sixty-nine and doesn't move fast. Also, she never really knew how to handle a phone properly. I only heard half of what she shouted; she heard almost nothing of what I said. But I *could* hear the time-counter clicking away and wondered how much this nonsense was going to cost me.

"What did you say?" my mother shouted.

She always shouts on the phone.

"I'm coming home."

"Speak louder, Eugène. I can't hear you."

"I'm coming home!"

Now I was shouting too.

"Home?"

"That's what I said."

"Wednesday?"

"Yes, Wednesday," I sighed. "Or maybe tomorrow."

"Taking a vacation?"

"No, Mom. I'm coming back for good."

Oh, what was the point of trying to explain anything to her?

"I can hardly hear you, you know, Eugène."

"I know, Mom. It doesn't matter. I'll talk to you when I get there."

"Yes!" she shouted uncertainly, like a deaf woman.

"Love you, Mom. See you tomorrow," I said.

"Yes."

"See you tomorrow!"

"Yes."

I hung up, bathed in sweat. I poured myself another pastis. It was only five in the afternoon, but I needed a drink.

When I calmed down, which didn't take long, I called the Gare de Lyon to get the train schedule. There was a train at 7:50 the next morning that wasted a ton of time cavorting about near Vierzon, but all in all it was the most convenient, and with any luck I'd be at home by late afternoon. I wrote it down. I poured myself another drink.

By dinnertime I was drunk, and it felt like a bocce ball had replaced my brain. I'd packed my bags—not much to do there—and written a letter to my landlord to say I was vacating the place and could I get my security deposit back and only pay for half of the trimester, seeing as I was leaving? He could pick the keys up from Stanislavski. I'd have the furniture removed before the end of the week. I thought a little longer to figure out if I wasn't forgetting someone to whom I should announce my departure. The answer was no, so I fixed myself a sixth pastis. That is, I didn't bother adding water; I just drank it straight. Not bad. Not as bad as a cobblestone chucked in your face. But I didn't want my thoughts to go down that road. I paced the apartment unsteadily. I would've liked to have a radio or television so I could revel in some show like everyone else while waiting to pass out. Dusk was falling and I opened the office window and saw it'd stopped raining. If I'd turned on the television instead of opening the window, I might have seen my mug. Except that they don't do reruns of the news.

Question: But before all that happened, you yourself were wounded?

Answer: Yes, precisely.

Q: Someone threw something at your face?

A: Yes, precisely.

Q: A cobblestone?

A: I believe so, yes, precisely.

Q: Did you panic?

[No answer. The camera stays a moment on the noncommittal (and ugly) face of the gendarme Eugène Tarpon, then cuts away to a rather sinister tracking shot of the barracks. Then . . .]

But my thoughts mustn't go down that road.

2

DOORBELL ringing.

I stood up. I'd been sitting dazed and crazed on the blue sofa. I ran wobbly legged to the desk, opened a drawer, and put my empty glass in it. I looked at my watch. Nine in the evening. I went to open the door.

In the hallway stood the silhouetted figure of someone young. It took a baby step into the vestibule and the lamp shed light on some things. It was a guy. He couldn't have been more than twenty. His hair was long and frizzy. He had an innocent looking face, at least that's the impression I got; all the booze in me was making me good-natured. He was wearing sailor pants, blue with white stripes, and a green suede safari jacket. And eyeglasses.

"Sorry to disturb you," he said. "Are you Mr. Tarpon?"

"In the flesh."

"I had to think twice about coming up. That's why... that's why I'm here at such a late hour..."

He cut himself off. His wires were crossed. I was still holding the door with one hand. Or rather, I was holding on to the door. So I wouldn't wobble.

"May I come in?" he said after a moment of reflection.

"What is it you want?"

He seemed confused.

"You're a private eye, aren't you?"

And there it was. That moniker straight out of a novel. I shrugged and stepped back. He came in. I didn't tell him it was over, that I was no longer investigating anything, that I'd never really begun. I was happy just to see someone.

He followed me into the office and I turned on the light in there. I let myself fall into the desk chair and pointed at the armchair for him. Then he sat down.

"What's the trouble?" I asked.

"My name's Alain Lhuillier," he said and then cut himself off again; he seemed to be waiting for something and after a moment I caught on. I opened several drawers, including the one with the empty glass, eventually found a pencil and paper, and wrote down his name. He seemed happy.

"What brings you to me? I mean, where'd you get my name?" I asked, thinking it was a good question. They often ask it in American movies, even though they phrase it better.

"You placed an ad in *Detection*."

"Yes, precisely."

I held on to the edge of the table and I felt like vomiting. *Yes, precisely*. I got a grip on myself.

"So," I continued. "What brings you here?"

"I'm the victim of racketeers. That is, well, it'd be best if I started at the beginning…"

He cast a tentative glance my way. I cast a sympathetic one his way. He went on.

"I opened a nightclub with some friends in the Fourteenth Arrondissement, just a small one. In theory it's a private club, but the fact is, it's open to anyone. It used to be a grocery store with a cellar. To tell the truth, I'm just the manager. Am I being clear?"

"Who owns the premises?"

"An old guy, I mean really old, a retired guy who left the

city. The grocery store was his and he couldn't find a buyer, so he gave it to my buddies and me. We didn't have much faith in the idea at first. We don't sell booze, you know? But I think it's the band that attracted so many people."

"Hold on," I said. "What band?"

"The Function of the Orgasm," he said, and my eyes grew wide, but he added right away: "That's the band's name, it's a jazz-rock band."

"Ah," I said, relieved, "a pop band."

"Not pop. Jazz-rock."

"Okay, fine. And?"

"Well, it started going really well. We opened in the fall and now we've got a full house every evening. We're making good money. Speaking of which, I'll have enough to pay you if you're not too expensive. I haven't asked you yet."

"We'll see. Tell me about the problem you're having."

He twisted around in the armchair to pull out a cigarette and I pushed the ashtray toward him. As he spoke, he tapped his cigarette more often than necessary.

"A month ago, two guys came in after closing time while we were cleaning up, two gentlemen in suits and all, respectable and oldish, tie and briefcase. You get the picture."

I did. Guys like all the other guys. He tapped his Gitane and continued.

"They said they represented a certain Old Age Insurance for Restaurant and Café Owners. Long story short, they advised me to contribute because it was supposed to offer a lot of advantages. When I told them no, they said it was mandatory. I started to get the picture and I told them to fuck off, see? They said they'd be back. I kept telling them not to bother. Long story short, the next evening when I went to open up the place, I wasn't thinking about them anymore, but I realized the place was already open, that is, it'd been broken into, and the amp was dead."

"The amp," I repeated.

To my knowledge, an amp was an amplifier, that is, a speaker inside a radio or a turntable. But the young man seemed totally devastated.

"The band's amp," he said. "Don't you know what that is?"

His gaze was filled with sorrow and pity. He explained that all the instruments were electric. All hooked up to the same amplifier, which had multiple inputs, multiple settings, and was as big as an armoire, and they couldn't play without it.

"And it was busted," I said. "I get it."

"Not to mention that we bought it used, see, but it still cost us five thousand francs."

"That's not such a tragedy."

"Five thousand new francs."

"Shit," I said.

He sat quietly in mourning for a few moments. Then he said, "The guys came back that same evening. You gotta believe me when I say I had to restrain myself from popping them one."

"You did the right thing," I remarked.

He practically snarled to show me how tough he was. It was odd, he should have seemed likable to me, but he was getting on my nerves. I'd had just about enough.

"They were very explicit. They wanted twenty-five percent of the profits or else it wouldn't be the amp they'd break, it'd be my hands. I'm the guitar soloist."

"Did you go to the police?"

"No."

"Can you tell me why? I'm not a mind reader, you know."

"I'm starting to realize that," he said. "I didn't go to the police because I knew if I did, the club would be fucked. The cops don't like us, so any investigation would just cause us problems, and the customers, my buddies and everyone, would've gone somewhere else."

All right, then, I thought.

"That was a month ago. So. You didn't go to the police. What happened next?"

"What do you think? I paid them."

"And you've had enough."

"Yes, because now they want fifty percent."

"They're nuts," I said. "They're going to bankrupt the place."

"They want me out, that's all. To put someone else in my place."

I should have thought of that. Suddenly I was furious at the young guy. I got up, took the empty glass from the drawer, and filled it with pure pastis. I emptied it. The young guy glared at me.

"Do you think I can do anything for you?"

"I'm starting to wonder."

Now he was becoming snippy.

"The answer is no."

He stood up, smiled scornfully, threw his cigarette down on the carpet, and crushed it calmly with his foot. I went to put my glass on the edge of the desk where it wavered and fell without breaking. I took two steps toward the young guy and grabbed him by the collar. He tried to push me away by sticking his fist in my ribs and I punched him in the gut, hard. He immediately doubled over, hiccupping. He was a lightweight. I was ashamed of myself. I was fighting hard against my shame. I didn't know how we'd gotten to that point.

"Fucking old asshole! Dirty cop!" he murmured.

Still holding him by the collar, I stood him up against the wall. My lips were close to his face. He was very pale; he looked like Medusa with his frizzy hair.

"Listen, tough guy," I said. "Don't try to fight. Get the hell out. And I don't only mean out of my place. Quit the club. Quit all of this shit. Hear me? There's nothing else to do. It's over."

"You stink of booze," he remarked. "You're completely drunk. Let me go."

I let go. I was panting.

"You're despicable," he said rather calmly. Then he left, closing the door without slamming it; I heard him go down the stairs.

Only once in my life had I felt worse.

After the kid had gone, I really started to drink.

I downed the whole bottle. What was left of it. Of course I felt sick. And the worst was every time the wave of nausea came over me again, I had to run to the toilet on the landing, bouncing and rebounding against the walls.

At last it was over and all I felt was a huge desire to pass out. I looked at my watch and saw that it was much earlier than I'd thought, not even eleven thirty. I set my alarm clock for six thirty, lowered the back and sides of the sofa bed, and took off the slipcover. I drew the curtains. I stripped to my underwear. I drank three big glasses of water in the kitchen and headed for bed, shutting off the lights behind me but looking at the place first and telling myself that this was the second to last time I would see it. I lay down, turned off the lights in the vestibule, and instantly fell asleep.

At midnight, I was woken by the doorbell ringing several times. Or rather, I was woken by one ring, but a whole series followed. I jumped out of bed, knocking over the pedestal table and the vase that still contained the water from the flowers. It pooled on the floor. I ran to the door and opened it. In the doorway stood a young woman in the throes of some very strong emotions. Because I hadn't turned on the lamp in my place, the yellow light of the hall illuminated her from behind, but I could distinctly make out the whites of her eyes and when she spoke, I noticed her teeth were chattering.

"Mr. Tarpon, don't you recognize me? Let me in, please. I'll explain."

She didn't wait for me to respond; she lurched inside, shoving me. I turned on the light. I realized I was in my underwear. The girl didn't notice. She was staring at me with bug eyes, lovely eyes in fact, but it was as if she were looking right through me. The feeling was so strong that I instinctively turned around and used the opportunity to close the door. So my back was to the girl and I didn't see her face when she said: "Griselda's throat's been slit."

I turned and leaned against the closed door and looked at the damsel in distress. She'd just sat down on my unmade bed and right then she must've felt faint; her face turned a greenish color, and she fell over and slid off the bed. She stayed sprawled out on the floor. I didn't think I'd ever seen her before. I decided to make some coffee.

3

IN THE kitchen, I made real coffee in a clay coffeepot with a paper filter. While it was dripping, I went back to the bedroom. The girl was wriggling about on the floor. I got into my trousers and shirt and put on a pair of clean socks.

"It's awful," said the girl. "She'd bled out completely. Someone slit her throat."

She raised her head and looked surprised to find herself on the floor.

"Would you like something to drink?" I asked.

She nodded vigorously and attempted to stand. She had to hold on to the bed and managed to do nothing but make my pillow fall down next to her.

"Don't move. You couldn't possibly sink any lower," I remarked, pulling out a pearl from my stash of old country wisdom. "Lean against the bed. I'll get you a drop of something."

Easier said than done. I knocked over everything in the kitchen cabinet and finally located a half-empty bottle of Kirsch Fantaisie. I must have bought it to do a little baking. I had to do *something* with my time during all those months.

I took in a tray with the kirsch, the coffeepot, and two mustard glasses and set everything down next to the girl. I looked everywhere but couldn't find my shoes. I felt a bit on the tired side.

The girl took the bottle of kirsch, unscrewed the metal top, and gulped down half the liquid straight from the bottle.

"Bahhhh!" she said, crinkling her nose.

A pretty nose, by the way. A pretty girl. Not my type. Rather kittenish, as they say. A classy little chassis, a small triangular face, nice golden skin, long brown hair falling across her shoulders. The rest could only be imagined because she was wearing a suit of light brown suede; and although the damsel liked her jackets on the tight side, because for the moment she was holding herself together about as well as a venetian blind in a hurricane, she looked like a sack of potatoes. But her ankles were slim, her wrists too. She was wearing an Obrey watch and her clodhoppers didn't come from the dime store either. No purse, but a plethora of patch pockets with topstitching on her suede suit. She dug around in one of them and pulled out a pack of Gauloises. She offered me one and I accepted it, and as she was looking for something to light it with, I bet she was going to produce a lizard-skin Ronson, but I lost the bet; she pulled out a matchbook and managed to scratch her bit of cardboard on the first try. Either she recuperated quickly or else she wasn't as devastated as she wanted me to believe.

"So," I said, "Griselda got her throat slit?"

She nodded down and up, bizarrely, and blew a double stream of smoke out of her nostrils. Her pupils looked normal.

"Who's Griselda?" I asked.

"My roommate. Well, it's not a room; it's an apartment. And I went in and I found her. It was disgusting. All the blood. She had..."

"... bled out, I know, thanks. Spare me the rest; my stomach's queasy. Did you call the police?"

She shook her head forcefully.

"I came straight to you."

It'd been my lucky day, and now it was my lucky night. Lucky me.

"Who are you?"

"Don't you remember me?"

She said this as if everyone remembered her, and maybe she was right, I couldn't tell, she was more doubled over than before; she'd brought her knees under her chin and was holding on to her ankles with her hands. She kept the cigarette between her teeth and the smoke was forcing her to squint. I shook my head; I didn't remember her.

"A little less than a year ago."

"A little less than a year ago," I said, "I wasn't in Paris."

"I know. You were a gendarme in Brittany. I came on the set when they were interviewing you. Don't make that face."

"I don't know what face I'm making."

I tried to relight my cigarette and realized it hadn't gone out.

"Okay, so," I said. "You were on the set. That doesn't explain why you're here."

"It does, kind of," said the girl. "You struck me, I mean I was struck by you at the time of that interview and I said to myself, huh, there's a person who's not as sleazy as the rest of them. And later, Hervé...You remember Hervé? The director?"

I nodded.

"Hervé mentioned you to me again, you interested him, he knew you had left the gendarmes and set yourself up as a private eye, like they say. He thought that was a good subject, you know, the kind of 'Where Are They Now' thing. What happened to that gendarme who left the force after a moral crisis? It's kind of quaint that you've become a detective. I talked him out of it, though, because you've got a right to be left in peace."

"You shouldn't have," I said. "I could've used the publicity."

"In any case, the bastards in the department would never have accepted it. As it is, they were hiding under some rock when your interview aired. Anyhow, I immediately thought of you when I got home and saw Griselda."

She shivered. I poured some coffee in the glasses. She asked me if I had any sugar, and I said no.

"Did a murder really just occur at your place?" I asked. "You're not joking?"

"Fuck no!" she said.

She had a lovely pink mouth.

"Call the cops now," I said.

"I can't."

"Of course you can. And you're going to. What's your name?"

"Ah, the gendarme is coming back to life," she said, but her tone was slightly querulous.

"Listen, kid." I was trying to be fatherly and offer good advice. "If there was a murder, or suicide, or who knows what, you've got to call the police, that's all there is to it. You don't go running to a private investigator. Not in real life. In real life, a private investigator deals with divorce, store security, and, when he has more prestige than I do, industrial spying. Not violent death. There's a telephone in the next room and you're going to pick it up and dial the cops. The operator will put you through to your precinct. Where do you live, by the way?"

She emptied her glass without answering, and she didn't answer after having emptied it either.

"It'd be better if I called them from home," she said, "if you really think I should call them. In any case, they'll need me on the scene. I suppose they'll want to question me."

She got up. She was firm on her feet, and once she'd unfolded her legs I saw that she didn't look like a sack of potatoes in the least. In fact, she was the prettiest little kittenish thing I'd ever seen. She was also a liar. I stood up, too. I was between her and the door and she didn't look thrilled about that.

"Call from here," I said. "They'll send a car to get you."

"Mine is downstairs."

"Call from here," I said again.

"Let me explain something to you," she said quickly. "They're going to lock me up. I'm the perfect fall girl. My fingerprints are everywhere, even on the knife that belongs to me, and I got blood all over me."

I raised my eyebrows. I didn't see any.

"I changed my clothes," she said pleadingly. "It's true, I was covered in blood. It was everywhere. And it's my knife. And I even have a motive."

I took her by the arm and pulled her toward the office.

"Listen," I said. "I let you waste a lot of time because I wasn't fully awake, and because I couldn't believe your slit-throat story, and because, to tell you the whole truth, I got very drunk last night and still have a lot of booze in my system. But now I'm not going to let you waste any more, and you're going to call the cops because the sooner they get involved the better it'll be for everyone except the killer."

She clumsily tried to free her arm and dug her heels into the carpet, stubborn as a mule.

"Cut it out, dirty cop, asshole," she said. "That's not the whole story. There are drugs in the apartment and bombs in the basement."

"Sure, I believe you," I said. "There's also stolen jewels in the fridge, counterfeit money in the attic, and the body of a Chinese man in a trunk with microfilm between his teeth. Pick up that phone."

"Fine," she said with a sigh and I had the feeling she was giving in.

She crossed in front of me as if she were heading to the phone, and grabbed me by the neck, surprising me. For half a sec I thought she was still acting out her private American movie and that I was about to get a big wet kiss. Nope. It looked like she was going to sit down on the floor, but instead I caught her foot in my nether parts and flew off the ground. I didn't know if it was judo or something else, but I landed face down against my electric radiator. It hurt. My legs were tangled in the wire from the desk lamp, which had fallen without coming unplugged, and I was a bit confused. Which slowed me down. She picked up the phone all right, the vixen, but to use as a hammer. She knew exactly where to strike. I was suddenly disconnected from the space-time continuum.

4

IT ALL came back to me when I opened my eyes and saw the ceiling. I had my doubts about the reality of the facts, but I couldn't doubt the facts. When I touched my head, it hurt so much that I couldn't put the entire blame on the pastis. In addition, I was neatly laid out on the floor, with my pillow under my head. I was in the office, which was dark. The door to the vestibule was open and the light was on in there. Almost immediately I checked to see if I was all in one piece and could sit up and then stand. My watch read three thirty, and it was night behind the curtains.

I surveyed the apartment. The premises were empty. The bottle of kirsch was in the vestibule to make me believe the reality of the facts, and my first move was to empty it. I shivered and almost died, but managed to stay upright and after a moment I felt better.

There was a message on my bed where the pillow had been.

"I'm sorry I hit you," I read on a page torn from my empty datebook, "but it wasn't possible for me to call the cops. Everything I told you is true, including the acid and the bombs, so you've got to understand. Too bad you won't help me. Again, sorry for knocking you out."

That's it. It was written with my ballpoint pen and signed "M.C." in big block letters.

I thought about lying down again with a cold compress and going back to sleep, but instead I pulled my suitcase from under the sofa, opened it, and dug out my address book. The address I was looking for was in there, and so was the phone number. I dialed and on the eighth ring someone answered in a furious voice.

"I'm sorry to disturb you, Ma'am, but I have to speak to Hervé Chapuis. It's urgent."

She asked me a question, and I answered 3:40, repeating that it was urgent, and who was calling she asked? Gendarme Eugène Tarpon. No, Ma'am, it is not a joke. Yes, I'll hold.

"What?" asked a man's voice a moment later, and I started my litany again, who I was and how sorry I was.

"But I need some information. It's an emergency."

"We're not in a democracy," declared Hervé Chapuis, "when ex-gendarmes allow themselves to disturb law-abiding artists at four in the morning."

"I never said we were in a democracy."

"Okay. Touché. What's the problem?"

"When you interviewed me, you remember? There was a girl who came on the set, a skinny little brunette skilled in hand-to-hand combat."

"Yeah, I remember. So?"

"I need her name and address."

"What for?"

"I can't explain," I said.

"Aye yai yai," Chapuis said. "You're confusing me, gendarme. If you'd said to me 'I want her, I just woke up bathed in sweat and I thought of her immediately, I have to possess her this very minute, it just came over me after a year,' I would've understood. But theses mysteries . . . I dunno."

Silence. I sighed.

"I really can't tell you," I said. "I don't want to hurt her, that's all I can say."

"Is it serious?"

"Yes."

Another silence.

"Sexual?"

I held the receiver tightly in my hand. Good Lord, who stuck me with such a bozo? I took a deep breath with the intention of barking out something biting, but the artist didn't give me the chance.

"Oh, fuck, after all, why not? Her name is Memphis Charles. Be careful, gendarme. The last time I tried to rape her, she scalded me with a hot toddy."

"Where on earth did a name like that come from?" I asked.

"She chose it herself," he answered and he gave me her address. "Now," he added, "hang up and let me worry myself sick. It's not every day I rat someone out to a gendarme. You'll call me back to let me know how it goes, right?"

"How what goes?"

He'd hung up. The guy is half-nuts.

I'd finally located my shoes. They were in my suitcase. Liquor kills, I thought as I did up my shoelaces, put a brown wool tie around my neck, and a suit jacket on my back. I checked that my ID papers were in my pockets. I went out.

I found a cab on boulevard de Sébastopol. Memphis Charles—what a name! Her place was in the Fourteenth Arrondissement. Too far to go on foot, and too early for the Métro. Just perfect for the late-night surcharge on cab fare.

The driver stopped on avenue du Général-Leclerc.

"It's on the other side of the street," he said. "Do you want me to cross over?"

"No, this'll do."

"Thirty-two francs."

"You're kidding?"

"Plus tip," he said cheerfully.

I must have disappointed him on that count. When I climbed out, he leaned out his window.

"I don't know why I do the night shift," he said to me. "When it's not muggers, it's cheapskates. Next time, you'll hoof it, daddy-o."

And he almost ran me over as he pulled out.

I was careful to wait until he was far away to venture out again on the deserted sidewalk. I crossed the avenue at a slow trot. Memphis Charles, if the director had not led me astray, lived in the "Villa Auguste Ventrée," which sat on a private lane with a chain across the entrance. The chain was unhooked and lying on the ground.

"Sir," said an authoritative voice.

A uniformed cop came out of the guard hut and, like a clever sheepdog, herded me inside the lane.

"Good evening, officer," I said.

"ID check," he answered. "Do you live here? I need to see your identification."

"I don't live here. I was just passing by."

There was a second uniformed cop in the hut. I took out my wallet.

"I was just passing by," I said again. "I was out for a stroll. I couldn't sleep."

"You were just passing by," the officer repeated. "You came in a cab, you were dropped off on the other side of the avenue, and you were just passing by."

He took my wallet from me because I was not moving fast enough as far as he was concerned and he leafed through my papers. There was a business card among them. E. TAR-PON, INVESTIGATIONS, SURVEILLANCE, DISCRETION. He smiled.

"I'm going to have to ask you to kindly come with me," he said.

His politeness was hard to stomach. He consigned my wallet to his pocket. He took me by the arm. He shoved me inside the property's surrounding walls. Once you'd gone through the narrow entranceway, you were in a large square courtyard with a lawn in the middle and bushes on the lawn. On all four sides above the flower beds there were five-story buildings. In one of the corners of the square, invisible from the entrance, a patrol car was parked in the alleyway and the residence on the ground floor was brightly lit. The window was open, and you could see figures moving around inside. There was a sudden flash. Near the front steps, uniformed officers were ordering the local bourgeois folk in their bathrobes to return to their homes, stating against all evidence that there was nothing to see.

On the way to the "villa," the cop and I passed an unmarked Peugeot 404 in which a plainclothes cop was speaking into a radio. My officer addressed his colleagues.

"This gentleman will wait here," he said. "Don't go anywhere, hear?" he said, turning to me and patting his pocket where my wallet was.

Two cops surrounded me and gazed at me with curiosity while their little buddy entered the apartment building. I leaned against the patrol car.

"Don't lean on that," said one of my guards.

"Why? Are you going to kick me?"

He pressed his lips together. I shouldn't have said that. I moved away from the vehicle. The cop didn't say another word, but he was watching me with his big brown eyes. He was a fat officer, big and fat. Nice rosy complexion. Jovial sort. The sort that doesn't kill except maybe on the opening day of hunting season. He reminded me of a bunch of friends I used to have. I turned away to gaze at what was happening in the lit apartment. The windowsill was positioned a little above eye level, so I could only see the upper part of the room: bookcases, a shelf without books on which sat a squat red candle; a giant photo of a pregnant black woman wearing a button on her stomach (NIXON'S THE ONE said the button); at the other end of the bookshelves, another poster, a print of a pop singer whose name escaped me. Geiger? Jaeger? Something like that.

I could also see a portion of the sidewall. It was white and spattered high up with blood from below. The blood was dry and brownish at the moment, but nonetheless it made me nauseous to look at it.

A police photographer entered my field of vision just then, turned his camera on something I couldn't see and that in all probability was lying on the floor, or on a low sofa below the brown spatter, and he took a picture of whatever it was.

"Okay," he said.

In the flower beds and on the courtyard lawn, two flashlights were moving slowly, aimed at the ground. Very methodically, it seemed to me. The sky was turning blue, but it was still totally dark in the courtyard. Just then, my initial guardian angel came out of the building with a young man in a raincoat whose hair was longer than mine.

"Here he is," said the uniformed officer, pointing at me.

The plainclothes guy held my closed wallet in one hand and was patting the palm of the other with it. He had a very big nose, bright dark eyes, and olive skin.

"Why was this window left open, for God's sake?" he asked, but the question wasn't for me. "Follow me, Mr. Tarpon," he added and headed back to the apartment building. I followed him.

The first door on the left in the entrance hall was open. He ushered me in and closed it. We found ourselves in a narrow hallway that had walls covered with jute and four open doors. They opened respectively onto a kitchen the size of a telephone booth, a bathroom just as enormous, and two bedrooms. The lights were on everywhere and several people with a tendency to bump into one another were roaming about. Sometimes the thought could cross your mind that cops are fatter than normal people.

Schnozzola carved out a path to the bedroom that overlooked the courtyard and I followed him while the police photographer and I elbowed each other as he was on his way out. I managed to enter the bedroom just as Schnozzola was closing the window taking all sorts of precautions, no doubt because of fingerprints. I looked at the inside of the room, which I hadn't been able to see from outside: the straw mat on the floor, the cushions to sit on, the two white plastic coffee tables, the sofa, and the dead young woman on the sofa.

Her hair was blond, but the roots were brown. She'd been voluptuous. A little too much so for my taste, but she must have pleased the lads with her big firm breasts, her large mouth, her dark eyes (wide open now, aimed at the ceiling, startled-looking), and the haunches of a broodmare. Her short black nightshift was in stark contrast to her milky-white skin, and it was unbuttoned from top to bottom. It had been opened brutally, because there was a button on the sofa and another on the floor. Her panties had been split in two, not torn but slashed with a sharp blade. The dead woman was not wearing a bra, and her throat was slit like you wouldn't believe. The killer had butchered her jugular vein and carotid artery, and the whole mess was horrific. The front of her body had been scratched and bitten, at least as far as I could tell at first glance from two meters away. Blood had spurted out in every direction; some had even dribbled down into her navel. The sight didn't make me want to throw up. It just gave me a feeling of deep mourning.

"Step back, step back, my God! Get out of here!" Schnozzola said, turning away from the window and rushing toward me.

"Sorry," I said.

I stepped back and exited the bedroom.

"You'd told me to follow you," I commented.

"Come in over here."

He had me enter the other bedroom, which was similar yet different, as they say in poems. From the doorway, he shouted various things at the people bumping into one another in the narrow corridor; he said the stretcher would never fit through there, and everyone finally agreed to evacuate the remains through the window. Meanwhile, I continued standing in the room and my guess was that it belonged to Memphis Charles. A low, blue sofa. White walls. Armoire. A kitchen table with a Formica top and stainless steel legs. On the table, a Philips record player with the lid lifted and a pile of records. The one on top was called *Seven Steps to Heaven*, which seemed to fit the bill, and was by Miles Davis. On the floor against the wall, next to the sofa, were books, a portable TV, and a plastic bag filled with hair curlers.

Two matching chairs flanked the kitchen table and some guy had set his fat fanny on one of them. He was holding a notebook and gazing at me malevolently. He was short and stocky, gray hair in a crew cut, square, symmetrical, clean-shaven face, small gray eyes. The other plainclothes cop, the young one, gently pushed me toward the table.

"Eugène Tarpon," he announced. "Private investigator, former member of the National Gendarmerie. Gamelin stopped him at the villa entrance. He arrived in a taxi and was dropped off across the street. He was about to come in. He claims he was out strolling."

"I'm not claiming that anymore," I said.

About that "former member of the National Gendarmerie": it wasn't written on my card. But he must have found it somewhere or other in my wallet, which was in fact splitting at the seams.

"Sit down, Tarpon," said the seated man.

I sat on the other kitchen chair. Schnozzola leaned against the wall next to the door.

"I'm Commissioner Coquelet," the other guy said. "And this is Officer Coccioli."

"Pleased to meet you," I said. "Criminal Investigation Division?"

He nodded.

"Okay," I said. I was waiting for whatever was supposed to come next, but apparently so were they.

"What brings you here?" Coquelet asked at last.

"I was visiting an acquaintance. Memphis Charles. A young woman, despite her name. I think it's a stage name. I don't know her very well."

"She's a whore," suggested Coquelet.

"How do you know her?" Coccioli asked almost simultaneously.

"As far as I know, she's not a whore. How do I know her? I . . . I was interviewed on TV last year, a show on the Gendarmerie, a news show called *The Depth and the Field*. Well, it used to be called that. It's off the air now. Anyway, Memphis Charles was on the set. We chatted."

"And that's how you wound up visiting her at night," said Coquelet.

"Eugène Tarpon!" exclaimed Coccioli.

The commissioner and I looked at him. He had a finger in the air. He calmed down.

"I wondered where I'd seen you. So. On TV."

"Yes," I said.

"You killed a man, didn't you? On duty. A farmer at a protest. In Saint-Brieuc, wasn't it?"

I nodded.

Someone knocked at the door.

"Yeah?" said Coquelet, annoyed.

"The body has been removed," announced the uniformed officer. "And we found a knife. Looks like it could be the weapon."

"Lemme see."

The uniformed officer signaled and murmured something into the minuscule entranceway and a plainclothes officer slipped into the room. He was the one I'd seen talking into the radio in the Peugeot a little earlier. He had a box in his hand. He held it out to the commissioner. It was open with a knife inside between cardboard wedges. The Laguiole inside was also open, completely sheathed in blood, both blade and handle.

"In the flower beds, next to the courtyard exit," said the plainclothes officer.

"Okay. You take care of the prints," said Coquelet, and the officer went back out with his box, and the commissioner began looking at me again with his beady gray eyes.

"So. You killed a man," he said. "Not nice."

"Let's not discuss it anymore," I said.

"And you chatted," he repeated, picking up the initial thread of our conversation. "And that's how you wound up visiting her at night. Memphis Charles, I mean."

He said Charles the English way, "Tcharles," not "Sharle" like in French. So very educated of him. He must have been externally recruited, which requires a degree to be promoted to commissioner. A rare bird. Personally, I have a hard time understanding guys who have no trouble with their studies and wind up being cops. But that's another story.

"You're mistaken," I said. "I know it all seems odd, and it's a damn coincidence in any case, that I got here right after…hmmm…what happened…But it's the first and only time I felt like coming to see the young woman. I had the blues. If you make me take a blood test fairly soon, you'll find alcohol. I got myself plastered."

"Why?"

"Huh?"

"Why did you get plastered?"

"I was depressed," I said.

"Why?"

"Oh, you're becoming a pain in the ass," I said.

He smiled as if he were pleased I was getting annoyed. He stood up. He was a little shorter than me. About one meter sixty-five.

"Tarpon," he said, "you know what has to happen. You arrived out of the blue. Naturally, you're a person of interest. It's obvious, no?"

"Yes, I see that."

"Added to the fact that you're a…"—He was going to use a swear word but he stopped himself in time—"private investigator or whatever. What do you expect me to think? That there's no relation? Were you summoned by someone? That Memphis Charles perhaps? Yes or no?"

"No."

He tapped his teeth with his pen.

"Suppose this Memphis Charles had something to feel guilty about," he said absentmindedly. "Don't you think she would have turned to you?"

"I've no idea. I don't know her well enough," I said. "But anybody who's normal sees what's happening next door and calls the police. Did she call you? Listen, if she had something to feel guilty about, she wouldn't have come to an ex-gendarme. Presumably, I'm on the side of the law, right?"

"There are two kinds of private detectives," said Coccioli. "Ex-cops and ex-cons. And sometimes it's hard to tell them apart. Judging by their actions."

"Good God," I said. "It's a murder we're talking about, not adultery. Nobody tries any tricks with murder."

"Where were you at the time of the crime?"

Asshole, I thought.

"What time was that?" I said.

"We don't know yet," Coquelet said with a sigh. "Say, you wouldn't know if your girlfriend Memphis Charles was on hallucinogenic drugs, now would you?"

"Hallucinogenic drugs?" I repeated. "LSD, stuff like that? No, I mean, I don't know. I told you I didn't know her well."

"A murder under the influence of drugs," explained Coquelet, "would be an extenuating circumstance."

Extenuating circumstance, my foot! So they did find some shit in her room. I felt a drop of sweat fall from my underarm and slide down my ribs under my nylon shirt. Did that mean the bombs in the basement were for real too? What the hell had I gotten myself into? I looked at Coquelet and was about to tell him everything in detail, because what the fuck did I care about that young woman anyway?

"Listen, commissioner," I heard myself say. "You're trying to pat me down everywhere to see where it rings hollow. I'm not one to reproach you for that, but I've told you everything and I'm rather tired. Don't you have other witness statements to collect, reports to come in? The autopsy, fingerprints, and all that? Meanwhile, I suggest you take me down to head-quarters and that someone record my statement according to procedure."

Coquelet stood up.

"It can wait until tomorrow. You're right, you must be tired. You look it, old man. Go home, get some sleep, and then I'll call you into the station."

I stood up as well. I looked at him. His expression was frank and open. I thought for a moment he was going to kick me or something, but he didn't.

"Give him back his wallet," he said to Coccioli.

The officer handed me the object and I pocketed it. I said goodnight. I went out.

I left the apartment without anyone stopping me. In the building foyer, the cops had opened a small low door under the stairway and halos were visible from the flashlights moving about in the depths.

"Tell the commissioner. He needs to see this," I heard.

I immediately turned around in the hallway and went through the little door.

"Hey, where do you think you're going?"

I went down the stairs. About fifteen cement steps. Then a slag floor under the soles of my shoes.

"Hey, you! Stop, goddammit!"

I arrived behind two uniformed cops who turned toward me, furious. But I could see, above their huge shoulders, a small cellar lit by a big electric lightbulb with a plank placed on sawhorses and six Molotov cocktails on the plank. Then they grabbed me.

"So sorry," I said. "Where's the fucking exit?"

A third cop came up behind me and did a half nelson on me to pull me backwards.

"Don't get riled up," I advised. "I took a wrong turn looking for the exit. That's not a crime."

I climbed upstairs with a little help. Back in the building hallway, I smoothed my jacket and brushed off my knees. Coquelet had come out of the apartment and was staring at me with a pained look on his face.

"You're drunk, it's true," he said. "Confusing the stairway to the cellar with the exit . . ."

"Do we book him for drunkenness, swearing, and resisting arrest?" asked the uniform who'd twisted my arm.

Coquelet shook his head.

"Let him go. He's a man broken by alcohol and regrets. Let him go nicely."

They made me leave the building with hard kicks to my ass.

5

OUTSIDE the dawn was breaking. Everything was bluish and coldish. The sky was overcast, with a few breaks in the clouds. The police van had left but another one had arrived. The Peugeot was still double-parked in the alleyway. The bourgeoisie had gone back to bed and the policemen were playing cards on the hood of a Renault 17.

"Don't lean on it," I advised them.

If the gaze that the brown eyes were sending my way had been a dagger, it would have stabbed me, as I think Jules Verne said (or something to that effect). Nonetheless, I strode across the courtyard without difficulty and reached the exit. I waved my open wallet under the nose of the two cops on duty.

"I've been authorized to leave. See, the bosses gave it back to me."

They didn't answer and I reached the sidewalk on avenue du Général-Leclerc. I hung a right. I walked toward the Alésia Métro stop. I heard a car start up behind me and follow me slowly. The engine was old. If that was the tail they were sticking on me, it lacked discretion.

But the vehicle ended up passing me a little before Alésia and pulled over near the curb, about ten meters in front of me, and the door opened halfway. I headed straight toward it. That's how you get killed in the movies. I opened the door all the way and no one emptied a gun in my gut. There was an old guy at the wheel who was almost as decrepit as his decrepit Simca Aronde. He was wearing a brown herringbone overcoat and a plaid scarf with a Prince of Wales cap on his head, which looked like the head of a noble father with a bit of satyr thrown in. He resembled the actor Jean Tissier.

"What do you want?" I asked.

"Journalist," he answered. "Can I drive you where you want to go?"

"Show me your press card," I said.

I wasn't sure the old warhorse was a cop. First of all, he was well past retirement age. Then he showed me a card that was well past its expiration date.

"It's well past its expiration date, Monsieur Jean-Baptiste Haymann," I said.

"I'm retired," he said. "Not working anymore."

"So what are you doing right now, then?" I asked commonsensically.

"Sit down and shut the door, for Pete's sake. It's cold."

I did as I was told and repeated my question.

"Bah," he said, starting the car again. "Reflexes, as they say. I'm bored stiff, get it? And when I'm bored, I go to the hospitals, the police stations, places like that. I don't sleep well and I don't want to take all the shit they prescribe you. So if some chamomile tea doesn't do the trick, I drive around. In case I come upon some scoop. Where to?"

"Huh?"

"Where we off to?"

He pronounced it "wofftoo." I didn't understand. I envy people who constantly display their wits for their own benefit.

"What did you say?" I asked.

"Where are we going?" he shouted in my ear.

"Ah! Straight ahead."

"Got anything to drink where we're going?"

"I'm not deaf," I said, because he kept shouting in my ear. "No, I don't have anything to drink. Why?"

"Because I'm thirsty."

"Sorry," I said.

"Let's go to Montparnasse," he decided. "There are a couple of cafés opening up at this time."

"I'm not going to Montparnasse. I'm going home."

He didn't answer and he turned down avenue du Maine. I gave up protesting. In any case, I felt like having a cup of coffee. It was getting on 6:00 a.m. and from time to time you could see a truck. A mud-covered Lancia roared past us.

"No paupers after ten at night," Haymann grumbled.

"Huh?" I said again.

"Nothing," he answered roguishly, but he kept talking anyway: "They drive around until dawn, the bastards," he said. "The bastards with money. The later it is, the richer they are. We live in a sick world. Haven't I seen your mug somewhere? You could introduce yourself, you know."

We were stopped at a red light. A very big truck pulled out of a very small street and passed in front of us, glorious in the bright morning.

"It's my lucky day. Everyone remembers me. Eugène Tarpon."

He squinted. The light turned green.

"Saint-Brieuc, wasn't it?"

Someone honked behind us.

"Yes," I said.

"Shut up, assface!" cried Haymann at a tomato-red Toronado that screeched past us.

He turned to me as we slid peacefully toward the Maine-

Montparnasse Tower, which was quite monstrous in the light of the rising sun.

"And what is it exactly that you do in life at the moment, Mr. Tarpon?"

"Investigation, surveillance, discretion, moderate prices."

"You're kidding!"

"I wish I were."

He began to laugh with a laughter that promised to be long but that didn't keep its promise.

"In regards to surveillance," he said, "have you noticed that we've been tailed since Alésia?"

"By a gray Peugeot 404?"

Haymann nodded.

"They're so childish," he sighed. "Want me to lose them?"

"With your Aronde?"

Ice-cold stare.

"Yes. With my Aronde."

"I believe you," I said. "But it's not worth the trouble. I've nothing to hide."

We turned down the departures road at Montparnasse station, unless it was the arrivals road; I can never tell them apart. We passed in front of the Inno department store and came out on the place de Rennes.

"Perhaps you still think I'm an inept cop," Haymann said. "I think I'd best take you home with me."

With that, he turned sharply onto the place de Rennes and sped down the other street, the arrivals one, unless it was the departures one, in any case, the other one, and he began to drive like a madman through the intersections.

"Is it far?" I asked.

"Five minutes."

At the speed we were going, in five minutes we could be

as far away as the other side of Corbeil. A good night's sleep would have been of more use to me than a lecture, but I didn't say anything. I turned halfway around and, through the rear windshield I saw the 404 in the distance running a red light to follow us. There was a tremendous din of horn blowing and a yellow Volkswagen Beetle sideswiped the Peugeot. Boom. The 404 zigzagged, climbed up on a sidewalk, and banged into a bus shelter. That's all I saw. I turned back to Haymann. He was smiling. I was almost sure he'd never been a cop because it seemed a truly harebrained scheme to have me get in his car, be tailed by another cop, then lose that one only to make me trust him. But I didn't say anything because if he wasn't a cop, I still didn't know what he was.

Ten (and not five) minutes later, we'd crossed through the Porte de Vanves, driven through Malakoff, and found ourselves in the suburb Clamart on a steep, leafy street with small front vegetable gardens behind grayish wood picket fences and ugly detached houses behind the vegetable gardens. Haymann stomped on the brake and slid the car up a cracked sidewalk. The Aronde stopped in a cloud of dust.

"You drive too fast," I said.

"That was nothing. When I'm drunk, it's really something to see," said Haymann, and he got out of the car.

He opened a wire mesh gate and then pulled in the Aronde. I got out of the car too and followed him along a yellow gravel alleyway until we reached a two-story cement house that must have been at most five meters long by five meters wide. The shutters were closed and Haymann opened them one after the other as he went through the rooms: a kitchen and an immaculate living room downstairs, a bedroom upstairs, with the bathroom on the narrow landing, and that was all.

Haymann wasn't smiling anymore; he was glowering. He opened a secretary desk in the bedroom, next to the cot, pulled out numbered cardboard files that were strapped closed with a strip of canvas and tossed them on the bed.

"Go ahead and search, you doubting dipshit, you."

I searched. Not for long. The files were filled with press clippings, articles signed J. B. Haymann that went back to 1935 and stopped in 1969. I retied the canvas straps. Haymann was standing next to the secretary desk. He tossed a little book to me, a small white volume published in Monaco. It was called *A Rolling Pen* and apparently contained his memoirs as a journalist. Okay. His photograph was on the back cover. Okay.

"So, are you reassured, Doubting Dipshit?"

"Can I make a call?"

He nodded and went down the stairs in front of me. He closed the living room door on me. Once again I called Hervé Chapuis. It was six thirty in the morning. He picked up this time and let out a cry of rage. I waited for him to calm down.

"Since you're a journalist, I thought I could ask you for some information," I said.

"Go fuck yourself. I'm not a journalist. I'm a director. What do you want to know?"

"Ever hear of a journalist named Jean-Baptiste Haymann?" I asked.

"No."

"Could you find out who he is?"

"Why are you persecuting me like this?"

"I've no one else to persecute. Can you find out?"

"Now?"

When I said yes, he started up with his cursing again. Then: "What do you want to know about the guy?"

"What his reputation is. If he can be trusted."

Silence on the line.

"Hello? Are you there?"

"Mm-hmm. You intrigue me, Tarpon. I hate you."

"I still can't explain anything to you. Can you find out and call me back?"

I gave him Haymann's number. He cursed at me some more. We hung up. I went back up to the bedroom where my retiree was waiting for me.

"So, Doubting Dipshit. Did you try to get some information on me?"

"Yes," I said.

"Are you going to tell me what happened in that villa where I met you?"

"Yes."

He'd brought up some coffee. It was very bad. With a drop of clear booze, the kind they sell by the liter to make liquor-infused fruit, it nonetheless warmed us up. We drank it. I told him about the girl with the slit throat, the hallucinogenic drugs in the apartment, and the Molotov cocktails in the cellar.

"The girl's name?" Haymann asked.

"I don't know," I said. "I thought I heard the name Griselda, but it seemed odd."

"Very Shakespearean," said Haymann. "You don't know her last name?"

"No, but I know her roommate's name."

I told him what I'd told to the cops. That I'd met Memphis Charles on the set of my interview, after Saint-Brieuc; that we'd chatted; that I'd taken down her address; that I'd decided to go over to her place because I had the blues; that I didn't know her.

"That's what you told them?" Haymann asked. "Bravo. And they let you leave? Oh, sorry, I get it. I see why you thought I was a cop. Who are the gentlemen in charge of the affair?"

"A certain Commissioner Coquelet."

Haymann nodded and emptied his cup. He poured in some more alcohol, without coffee this time.

"He's an intellectual," he said. "His trick is to let you go in order to trap you later. That's his modus operandi. He knew right away you were in contact with the other girl, the roommate..."

"Memphis Charles," I said. "But that's absolutely false."

"You lie like a rug," Haymann stated. "It doesn't matter. Memphis Charles, huh? May I make a call?"

He left the bedroom without waiting for my answer, went down the staircase, and shut himself in the living room. I went down behind him and listened at the door. I think he called Agence France-Presse, and he asked for someone he knew, a theater and TV expert apparently.

"A certain Memphis Charles," he said. "Memphis as in Tennessee and Charles as in De Gaulle. She must work in TV or something like that. No, I'll hold. But there's something else. Her friend too, but I don't know her last name. Griselda something. Same address, yeah. Thanks."

I unstuck my ear from the door, with a sense of relief because I felt like I had egg on my face spying on him like that. I went back upstairs. Haymann came up a little later with a piece of paper where he'd written down some things. I was on my third coffee. The coffeepot was empty. I had heartburn.

"Here we go!" Haymann cried with painful optimism. "The victim called herself Griselda Zapata. No more Zapata than you or me. She was born Louise Sergent on January 3, 1945, in Courville, near Envermeu, Seine-Maritime. Actress, supposedly. Small roles in things titled *Forbidden Caresses*, *How to Cure a Homosexual Without a Hassle*, and, hold on to your hat, *The Desires of the Tartars*. You have very interesting friends."

"I didn't know her," I insisted. "Only her friend. And barely."

Haymann sat back down and poured himself some alcohol again. He gestured to me to help myself, but I shook my head.

"Memphis Charles, huh?" he said. "That's not her real name either. Her name is Charlotte Schultz. Also an actress, and a stuntwoman. Cleaner than her friend. Born in Paris in '53. Stuntwoman in tons of things and small roles in other underground things. You can thank me."

"What for?"

"For the information. For the continuation of your investigation. A toast!"

He drank.

"I'm not investigating anything," I said. "I'm not crazy. There's been a murder. Not my thing."

He shrugged.

"Personally, I would find it fantastic to investigate," he said.

"Go for it," I said.

"Would you want me to keep you informed if I did?"

"Well, I suppose," I grumbled.

The phone rang. Haymann frowned and looked at his watch.

"It's most likely for me," I said.

We went down together. It was for me; it was Hervé Chapuis.

"Your Haymann is an old man," he said. "A pain in the ass, apparently. But straight as an arrow. Is that what you wanted to know?"

"I think so."

"What's going on, Tarpon? Is there some relation to Memphis Charles?"

"If you happen to see that one, tell her to call me."

"What the heck is going on?" he said again.

I would've liked to know.

6

HAYMANN drove me back home. On the way, I asked him how he happened to have been there in front of the Villa Auguste Ventrée when I'd come out. He gave me a sidelong glance.

"Now you don't think I'm a cop anymore, but you're wondering if I'm not a sadistic murderer," he said.

I responded that I was just gathering information, nothing more.

"I was at the police station in the Fourteenth Arrondissement," he explained. "I told you, I was bored stiff, I couldn't sleep. I went to see the cops. They know me. Then I went to see the young guys, the freelance journalists. You know, there are a few of them left, that race of youngsters who go to hospitals and police stations in the hopes of finding a scoop? Well, in any event, I was drinking some mulled wine with the guys, the cops I mean. And with a couple of young stringers who left at around eleven thirty to check out some brawl among black folk near the Porte d'Orléans. Obviously I'm not very interested in brawls. So I stayed there drinking mulled wine trying to teach those idiots how to play poker when someone called around midnight. It seemed it was a woman saying that someone was fighting on the ground floor of the villa, two girls pounding each other."

"Two girls," I said.

Another sidelong glance. The Aronde was heading north on boulevard Saint-Michel. We passed a garbage truck with a few third-world types hanging off the back. The day promised to be even colder than the previous one. All their bullshit about a dying planet could turn out to be true in the end.

"Yeah," said Haymann. "Two girls. It's not surprising that Coquelet wanted to have you followed. He wanted to find that Charlotte Schultz. You wouldn't know if he found any other incriminating stuff against your protégée?"

"She's not my protégée."

"So you say. Still. You wouldn't know something?"

"Nothing," I said, and I thought about the knife and I wondered what motive she'd alluded to. I tried to imagine Memphis Charles, formerly Charlotte Schultz, coming to ask for my help at midnight, having planned to knock me out with the phone, then returning to her place immediately afterward to commit the murder she'd told me about beforehand as if it had already occurred, then skipping town in the hope that I'd be her alibi; it didn't make sense, or I simply couldn't make sense of it. I leaned back against the headrest and sighed.

"Nothing," I repeated. "And then?"

"What, and then?"

"A woman called to say that two women were fighting. And then?"

"Oh. Okay. The woman hung up when they asked for her name. The guys sent a patrol car over there and, well, I hadn't paid much attention until then, but they discovered the murder and all hell broke loose at the station. Then the guys wouldn't talk to me anymore. The bastards. All of a sudden they went all by-the-book on me and almost threw me out. I won't forget."

"What about the woman who called? Did they find her?"

"Not to my knowledge."

"So," I said. "Then what?"

We were passing in front of the courthouse.

"So I wanted to see what all the commotion was about. But I'd wasted time. When I got there, it was too late. They wouldn't let me go in. I waited. You know the rest."

I hoped so. I didn't say anything in response. We raced down boulevard de Sébastopol. Ever since they got rid of Les Halles, you could drive faster. That's what I'd heard, in any event. I wasn't here when Les Halles were.

"Turn right," I said. "Your first right. There. Stop!"

Haymann dropped me off in front of my place. It was almost eight in the morning. My head was killing me and I was tired. I didn't feel capable of thinking. I said goodbye and thanks to the old journalist.

"You'll keep me posted, won't you, Doubting Dipshit?"

"Okay. If you'll do the same. You've got good people skills. I might need them."

"So you're going to investigate?"

"I don't know. Do you believe me?"

He looked at me and shrugged.

"Fine. Ciao," I said.

We exchanged phone numbers. I climbed up to my apartment, and the five flights of stairs were torture. No one was waiting for me on the landing, not even Coquelet or one of his stooges. I went in and bolted the door. Memphis Charles's message was on the desk where I'd left it. Not very clever of me. I burned it in an ashtray and I dumped the ashes down the drain. I was dying to go to bed, but instead I did a bunch of little things. Fresh pot of coffee. Sent a phoned telegram to my mother to tell her I wasn't coming today. I drank the

NO ROOM AT THE MORGUE · 51

coffee at my desk and I started thinking, lulled by the sound of Stanislavski's sewing machine. My thoughts went nowhere. I put down my cup, stretched out on the sofa bed, and immediately fell asleep.

7

I OPENED my eyes, got out of bed, went into the office, glared at the phone, and picked it up.

"Hello? Is this Mr. Tarpon's office?"

A voice from the backwoods. He too was screaming into the phone.

"Yeah," I grumbled.

"Mr. Tarpon the detective?"

I looked at my watch and I thought shit because it said three o'clock and it was undoubtedly the afternoon. That'll teach me to overdo alcohol, exercise, or work. Work! Hah!

"Yeah."

"In person?"

"Yeah. Who's speaking?"

"I gotta see you."

"Who are you, sir?"

"Gérard Sergent. I'm Louise's brother."

"Louise who?"

"For God's sake!" the idiot screamed. "My sister Louise who was stabbed by the sadist!"

Louise Sergent. Griselda Zapata. Aha. I was winning the prize for best idiot.

"Oh, yes," I said in a voice that was trying to transmit commiseration. "Louise. And you're her brother. And you want to see me."

"Yes. I gotta. I just came from the morgue. I'm with a friend of yours. A Jew."

He'd put his lips right against the receiver to whisper those last two words. How charming.

"I see," I said. "Haymann."

"That's the one. The police don't want to tell me anything, but he said you'd talk to me and it wouldn't cost that much."

Oh really? I was about to rip off a grieving hillbilly, or maybe he was a wealthy pig dealer.

"I'll be waiting for you," I said. "Do you have my address?"

"Yes."

"Okay. Let's say three forty-five."

"Fine."

"Please accept my condolences."

"Thank you."

He hung up. I hung up too and wondered how much money I could take him for. Still wondering, I went down to buy some aspirin and the evening paper. A small photograph of Griselda Zapata was on the front page. The deceased was wearing black thigh-high boots and frayed shorts, holding an angora cat in her arms to hide her breasts. MURDERED STARLET read the caption. "The murderer could be a burglar (see page 5)." Why not, after all? A burglar, or else an Apostolic nuncio, or else someone who knew the victim. Or even Lee Harvey Oswald. Someone like that.

"Mr. Tarpon?"

I was about to unfold and refold the paper in order to read the article on page 5. I stopped what I was doing. My heckler was thin with a pale face, a bluish chin because of his very virile beard, inky-black hair, and a plum-colored suit very tight at the crotch. I thought I'd seen him once or twice around the neighborhood.

"Whaddya want?" I asked.

"It's not me, it's my friends. They have some things they'd like to tell you. If you'd be kind enough to go to the hotel right next to your place."

"Right, son. Tell your friends to call me to set up an appointment."

I gently pushed him aside and went on my way. He followed me calmly, a few steps behind. I suppose he was thinking.

"I swear on my mother's life," he said at last, "I'm going to mess you up good if you don't come with me."

I looked at him. He'd taken a fur knife out of his pocket. It's not a weapon, it's a tool; you don't need a permit. Still, it can cut. What got into him to swear on his mother's life? The vein in my temple throbbed.

"Oh, it's that important, is it?" I said. "Fine. Let's not fight. I'll go."

He let out such a sigh of relief that he truly worried me. He'd really have done what he said if I hadn't agreed.

I walked toward my place, folding my paper in four and placing it under my arm. I turned to go through the entrance of the small hotel, passing the black plaque with its golden letters that advertised rooms by the hour or the day. A twenty-year-old lady who looked thirty thrust her flesh in my face.

"Let him through," the pale pimp ordered, and she sighed, which deflated her chest and simultaneously gave us room to pass.

I climbed up the stairs. When I got to the landing, I glanced at the deserted hallway and then turned back toward Loverboy. I kicked him in the nose. He fell backwards on the steps and, before he slid down, I jumped up and landed on his stomach with both feet. He made an awful sound, nothing but a consonant with no vowel behind it because he was gasping for air, and he began to slide down the stairway like a sled, and I was squatting on top of him and sliding down with him, like in Cinerama's *Seven Wonders of the World*. His head went "boom" against the entrance hall tiles when we got down to the ground floor.

"Oh, so that's what they're up to!" grumbled the impure vestal virgin of the amazing lungs. "I'm outta here," she added, and she left.

I pulled Loverboy up to standing position as he mumbled "G! R! K!" while scratching his throat, his mouth wide open and his face the same color as his suit. In addition, I'd broken his nose. He was going to love me his whole life.

He attempted to take out his slicing instrument, and I grabbed it from him. There wasn't a soul in that hotel. It was odd, but it was helpful. At the time, though, I didn't find it bizarre.

"What's your name?" I asked.

He tried to bite me. I banged his head against the wall.

"What's your name?"

"César."

It fit him like a glove fits a foot.

"Listen up, César. Your friends want to talk to me. I'm willing to listen to them, but I'm not willing to be threatened. Where are these friends of yours?"

"You're a faggot," César said. "You got me because I was thinking about something else. Wait till we meet again. I'll take you on whenever, however, wherever you want. And I'll make you eat your single ball."

"Of course," I said patiently. "Where are these friends of yours?"

"Upstairs."

"Be precise, or I'll fix your wagon."

"Fuck you."

"You want me to disfigure you for good?" I asked.

We exchanged a few more pleasantries of this kind.

"Room three," he finally said.

"How many are they?"

"Two."

"Who are they?"

"No idea. Hey! Don't do that! It's the truth, I swear, I don't know. I was told to do whatever they asked but I don't know them. Those faggots are not even French."

I let him go. I kept his knife in my hand. He immediately touched his nose and grimaced in pain.

"Bitch," he said. "I'll find you again."

"Don't cry, César," I said. "At least now you look like a real tough guy."

He spit on me. I wiped off my jacket as I climbed up the staircase. From above, I glanced back at him. He remained leaning against the wall, one hand on his nose, staring into the void. He smiled; he must have been thinking about my mutilated corpse. I sighed. I'd hit him because he scared me, that's true, and for no other reason. Nothing to be proud of. I walked down the deserted hallway to room three. I turned the knob and kicked the door open. The two guys inside stood up in a flash.

"Eugène Tarpon," I said wearily. "You wanted to see me?"

They were both very tall, thin, uniformly tan (sunlamps, I thought), but their features were drawn. Dark blue silken suits from the same tailor. Dark crew-cut hair. The one wearing shades took a small automatic pistol with a big silencer from his side pocket and aimed it at me with his arm outstretched. I hadn't foreseen that at all.

"Where's César?"

He had a foreign accent. American.

"Downstairs."

He raised his eyebrows (they appeared above the black frames of his sunglasses).

"Come," he said.

"Where?"

"You'll see."

He didn't leave me a choice as he walked out of the room. He kept me covered with his weapon, which was a .22 caliber Ruger—it was written on the gun. His buddy came out as well and patted me down. He took the fur knife, my ballpoint, my watch, and my keys. I had nothing sharp left on me. The buddy took me by the elbow. I walked on in the direction the gentlemen requested. I couldn't see how I could do otherwise.

We went into another room at the end of the hallway. A glass door led to an outside stairway that went down into a dark courtyard. We crossed the courtyard, then went through another building, and ended up in a back alley. Shades had put away his gun and I wanted to try my luck. Right when I was flexing my muscles to free myself, Shades grabbed my neck and used his body to twist my arm near the bottom of my biceps. I groaned. I was helpless. They don't teach us charming things like that in the Gendarmerie.

A tomato-red Toronado that I'd seen already somewhere was parked half on the sidewalk. The guy at the wheel and the other guys were like three peas in a pod. We climbed into the car. It pulled away, came out on rue Saint-Martin, and headed south. I looked at the Omega watch on Shades. Twenty to four. I was still helpless. I wasn't going to be on time for my appointment with Gérard Sergent.

8

THE DRIVER of the Toronado was polite and careful behind the wheel. You could tell he was someone who knew the value of rules. All around us, family men and decent citizens were risking their lives to shave five minutes off their commute. Not my guy. His 6:00 a.m. honking and his way of screeching past Haymann's Aronde must have been to make him seem normal, so he wouldn't get noticed tailgating us like some chump. Was I supposed to imagine that next, while we were losing the coppers' 404, racing to Clamart and back, the man had managed to flit around us without being noticed?

In that case, he was an extraordinary artist. I looked at his neck. He didn't have the neck of an artist. He had the neck of a businessman. Which didn't prove anything.

We drove out of Paris through the Porte d'Orléans (via rue Saint-Jacques, etc.) and it didn't take long for us to end up in the Verrières woods. The Toronado left the road to go down a muddy alleyway. And I still couldn't do a thing; the Ruger was pointed at my heart.

We stopped under the trees. There were leaves on the ground and buds in the air. Nature's great life cycle. And my life cycle? Were they going to interrupt it or what?

The driver opened his armrest and picked up a phone. A moment later, he started talking foreign into the thing. All that I could grasp was "Okay." Not much. He hung up and snapped the armrest shut.

"We wait," Shades announced. Five minutes later a Mercedes as big as a boat arrived—a model of limousine that seemed custom built to me, with a steel gray body and a TV antenna above the trunk, and curtains almost everywhere. It also turned down the muddy alley and pulled up alongside us.

"We get out," Shades ordered.

He only knew how to use the present indicative tense in French. Still, he managed to make himself understood. We got out. My three fellows still weren't giving me a break. We walked over to the Mercedes, sinking in the fallen leaves. There were no handles on the outside of the iron-gray doors. As we approached, one of the back doors opened, and the driver of the Toronado let go of me and spoke to someone in the Mercedes, someone we couldn't see because of the curtains. Then he turned to us and nodded.

"You get in this Mercedes," Shades said to me.

He pushed me toward the door with his left hand. The driver of the Toronado opened the door for me. I got in.

There was a partition glass between the back and the front seats of the limo. There was a window open in the partition. In the window was the barrel of an automatic pistol pointed at me by the driver of the Mercedes. A Beretta, it seemed to me, a small caliber one, probably a .22 again. Those goons adored their .22's, that is, they were overconfident or they had really good aim. I was leaning toward the second hypothesis because I'm squeamish.

I sat down carefully on the yellow leather seat, looking at the driver of the Mercedes, who had a blond crew cut, brown eyes, a thin nose, an expensive gray suit, and a nasty air about him. Someone shut the door on me and I saw that there wasn't a handle on the inside either. I wondered how a person was supposed to open it.

Next, I turned my attention to the man who was sitting in the back seat with me, and I want to say way down at the other end of the back seat because that rattletrap was truly vast.

He was a gentleman at least fifty years old; his body and skull were both ovoid. His arms and legs were small. His wide, pink hands had fat little fingers. One of his hands, the left one, was resting on the gentleman's knee, the other was holding a dirty handkerchief and dabbing the gentleman's eyes. His eyes were red and swollen. Tears were flowing freely from them. An allergy, perhaps?

He had a Bourbon nose and his chin was drowning in neck fat. The gentleman was bald as a cue ball, with a thick black paintbrush moustache. He was really very small, probably no taller than a meter sixty. His black suit appeared not to have been ironed for ages; his shoes were dusty, his socks were of white silk. His dingy shirt was one of those with a detachable collar worn by waiters, but he had neither collar nor tie. He made a very bad impression on me. He looked like an eccentric bum, something like a former high-level civil servant from the Ottoman Empire fallen on hard times but nonetheless equipped with a Mercedes. It made no sense. I had a sense of total senselessness. I senselessly tried to look all the way down the very long Beretta barrel. Then I turned my eye again toward the Ottoman detritus. He was looking at me and continued to weep abundantly. Time passed.

"So?" I said.

"Hush!" went the driver.

As for the detritus, he did not react. He was staring at me intensely and he was crying. Nothing else. He'd even stopped patting his face, and the tears were dribbling down it, catching in his beard, which was twelve hours old and white; then they trickled down his double chin and disappeared into his collarless shirt. I felt particularly uneasy.

I waited.

After five or six minutes, or two hours, or two years, the detritus touched his face with his left hand. He palpated his damp cheeks and his beard, still staring at me. The white of his dark eyes was bloodshot. He must have been crying for some time.

He leaned forward, reached with his left hand, and opened a compartment in the front seatback, next to the small television that wasn't broadcasting anything. He took out a battery-operated razor and turned it on. He shaved.

He was still looking at me. He was making the faces one makes while shaving; he stretched his throat to smooth out the skin, he pulled on the rolls of fat with his fingers in order to mow down every hair, and he stared at me obstinately, crying obstinately, silently, abundantly. He was giving me the creeps.

When he'd finished shaving, he put away his razor and I had the feeling that he blinked for the first time. His small fatty lips moved; they formed words but I hardly heard a whisper. Immediately afterwards the detritus seemed to settle down. He lost interest in me and stopped staring at me. The Mercedes driver made an eloquent sign with the Beretta barrel. I got out of the car. The daylight hurt my eyes. I wondered for how long I'd been in the dark.

Before Shades shut the door again, I saw the detritus turn on the TV. He was still crying. Then the door closed, the Mercedes started up, turned among the trees, went back down the muddy path, and disappeared.

"You walk home," Shades said.

His buddy threw my watch, my keys, and my ballpoint pen in the fallen leaves. The two of them and their driver got back in the Toronado and took off. I noted the license plate number, as I had done for the Mercedes; they were French plates. I put all that in a corner of my brain. I must have still been in shock because I jumped when the propeller of an Alouette II, out for a ride above the trees, pierced my eardrums with its infernal racket. I shook myself off, picked up my things, and started walking like Shades had told me to. It was five o'clock in the afternoon.

9

A BUS DROPPED me off in Sceaux. I took the train, transferred at Denfert, and arrived home by Métro in the middle of an ocean of exhausted, aggressive workers. On the streets, the cars were bumper to bumper and the air was horrid. The sun was shining for a change, so it was doubly suffocating. Still, I managed to make it back to my building and climb up the five flights of stairs. I was starting to die of hunger because I hadn't eaten a thing since my two eggs and piece of cheese thirty hours earlier. Luckily, I lost my appetite when I got to my landing because I saw Coccioli in front of my door. He seemed unhappy and had a bandage on his forehead.

"Where'd you disappear to, Tarpon?"

"I was in the woods."

"What did you say?"

"I was walking in the woods," I sighed. "Do you want to come in?"

I pulled out my keys. He shook his head, furious.

"You have to remain available to the police," he stated.

"I do my best," I said. "You should tail me. It would be safer."

If he'd had stitches, his irritation would have made them burst. I thought he was going to bring me in, but he calmed down.

"Aren't you the clever one," he said. "Bravo. You're right. Take advantage of everything life has to offer, Tarpon. You never know how much shit will hit the fan tomorrow."

I opened my door.

"And my formal hearing?" I asked. "Will it be soon?"

"The judge will hear you in due time."

"Fine," I said. "Coming in?"

He shook his head and strode down the stairs. I listened to him go. I shut my door. My windows overlook the courtyard. Too bad, I would've liked to know what car he was using to stake me out. It wasn't the 404 in any case. There mustn't have been much left of that one. I reached for the telephone to call Haymann and the thing started to ring as soon as I touched it.

"Mr. Tarpon?"

"Speaking."

"Hello, Mr. Tarpon. This is Mr. Stanislavski."

I asked how he was doing. He said he was doing perfectly well.

"I have two gentlemen here upstairs. They're waiting for you."

"I'm coming up."

I rushed to my suitcase under the sofa bed. At the rate things were going, I knew anything could happen. I opened an old candy box and took out my personal weapon, which is a P 35, that is, a Browning manufactured in Belgium by Poles under the German occupation. A real piece of poetry. I have a permit to own it but not carry. I stuffed it into my jacket pocket and climbed up to the sixth floor.

Stanislavski opened the door. He's a small wrinkled man, very badly dressed for a tailor. But nice, and there are very few people in the world about whom you can say that.

He didn't seem frightened, but I said to myself that there could be an entire team of assassins in the room, given how, as I said, I knew anything could happen at the moment. I almost knocked Stanislavski over to go in, my hand on my gun. Sitting on the workshop bench I saw Haymann and a fat young man who must have been Gérard Sergent.

"I see," I said.

"What's going on with you, Mr. Tarpon?" Stanislavski asked.

"Excuse me."

I took my hand out of my pocket and twisted it idiotically. I no longer knew what I was supposed to do with it. As a last resort, I extended it toward the fat young man, who stood up licking his lips and pumped my hand.

"Eugène Tarpon, Gérard Sergent," said Haymann, by way of introductions.

At the same time, he tapped his wristwatch with his index finger and gave me an exasperated, questioning glance.

"I'm sorry to be late," I said to Sergent.

"It's okay."

"You were out gleaning information, I'm sure," Haymann said peremptorily, nodding his head convulsively in my direction.

"That's it," I said. "I was gleaning."

Haymann took a step toward me.

"We were waiting in front of your door when we heard someone coming upstairs. I glanced in the stairway and saw it was Coccioli with his face like a bucket of smashed crabs, so we went up a flight. He stopped at your place, rang the bell for a while, and then waited some more. We couldn't go back down because the police have to stay out of all this, as I explained to our friend..."

He patted Sergent on the shoulder. I looked at the young man while Haymann was talking. He was really more on the short and stocky side than fat. Very wide shoulders that his nylon shirt and his suit jacket could barely contain. Prince of Wales. Ugly yellow shoes on his feet. A black knit tie around his neck. He was about my height, but took up at least twice the space. In his fat blond head were two round, faded blue eyes blinking beneath tufts of short lashes. He looked more like a cowhand than a pig dealer. He must have been broke. He didn't look like his sister.

"And then," Haymann concluded, pointing to Stanislavski, "this gentleman heard rustling on his landing, opened the door, and I whispered to him that we were waiting for you and he asked us in for tea."

The old journalist wiggled the glass he was holding, and it contained a liquid almost as clear as water.

"I made some for you too, Mr. Tarpon," the valiant little tailor added.

He took out a mustard glass, put some damp tea leaves in the strainer that he placed on the glass, and poured hot water through it.

I continued to examine Gérard Sergent as he sat back down, and then Haymann sat down next to him, and I grabbed a chair. No, the hillbilly didn't look like his sister, but I understood her better through him. And I wasn't surprised by what he said about her as we were drinking our tea.

"She was three years older than me and she wasn't a tramp at first, honest," he said.

He put his glass on the floor, pressed his fat red hands onto his spread knees and shot me a look as if daring me to say the opposite. I nodded. Stanislavski disappeared discreetly into the other room. He must have been working on something. Artisans like him must work every minute of the day just to survive. I would gladly have offered to go back down to my place to let him work in peace, but Sergent was warming up as he spoke, and then, I think, Stanislavski was happy to have a private detective in his workshop.

"And even later," said Sergent. "She stayed pure, you know. All these men were running after her, but she stayed pure."

"Which men?" I asked.

He didn't answer right away. He started talking about their childhood. And how happy he was back then. I thought to myself that the Envermeu region must have been idyllic, given his ecstatic-angel look when he talked about chickens and pigs.

"What did your father do?" I asked.

His gaze clouded over.

"I didn't have time to get to know him. He died when I was only two months old."

"Sorry to hear it."

"He left us the house and a bit of land, see. We weren't 'specially rich, but we were okay because we were fine, the three of us, Louise, Mom, and me, we didn't ask for anything."

"And then a man came from the city," I said in a sugary voice.

I almost could have told his story myself. He nodded and his ruddy face grew even redder. He was going to tell me again that his sister was pure. And bingo.

"She didn't understand," he explained. "She was happy to go out with him, for him to buy her things. And then when he asked her to work for him, she was happy too, to go to the city and all that."

Haymann and I exchanged a look. He seemed weary and fed up. Maybe he just didn't like tea.

Sergent went on talking. About how his sister had become an usher in the Coliseum movie theater in Gournay-en-Bray, because the guy owned the place. And how she accompanied said guy on his business trips to Paris.

"She met bad people," Gérard sighed. "'Cause the guy, he had what you call, uh, a film club, see? One night a week, he showed movies, uh, Swedish ones. Get it? That's why. She met people who rent that kind of movie. She didn't see anything wrong with that, but I know that they were all after her like dogs. I've gotta tell you that people who work in movies are almost all foreign shysters."

He interrupted himself and bit his lip, glancing at Haymann awkwardly. The old guy didn't flinch. He downed his tea in one gulp.

"Sorry," said Sergent. "I didn't mean that being a lech and not being truly French are one and the same."

"Stop floundering and finish your story," Haymann said smoothly.

"But you do see what I meant?"

Haymann got up and went to lean his forehead against the window overlooking the courtyard. His back was to us. Sergent looked at me as if he were begging for me to understand him.

"The Yid just gave you some good advice. Go on."

He grew purple and had a hard time finishing his tea, but he calmed down fast. He went on. His sister moved to Paris in the end, and she kept company with those . . . those gentlemen who work in the movies, and the gentlemen promised her a great future in cinema, and she had started to act in small movies.

"What kind of movies?"

"Small ones," he repeated stubbornly.

"Can you give me a few titles?"

He waved his big red hands around in despair.

"*Forbidden Caresses*," I suggested. "She acted in that one, didn't she?"

"Yeah, yeah. But she was . . ."

"Pure, I know." (I forced myself to smile at him because he may have suffered enough, and maybe it wasn't his fault that he was stupid.) "Don't wear yourself out," I said. "I know what movies she acted in. There's nothing wrong with that. You have to start your career somewhere."

"Personally, I was against it." He wanted to make that clear. "But as long as she remained pure . . ."

"And even if she'd had a little affair here and there, you can hardly blame her, can you?"

He gritted his teeth. I heard them grinding against each other.

"I'm positive she didn't," he said. "She would've told me."

"Did you see each other often?"

"She'd come to visit us in Courville, and sometimes I'd come to Paris. She'd bring us presents, Mom and me. She never forgot us. Sometimes when she didn't have time to buy us things herself, she'd send us money. Just to let you know what kind of a girl she was."

"A good little girl," I sighed.

"Better than you think," he said, looking me in the eyes, and I couldn't hold his gaze because after all, she was dead, murdered in a sordid way.

"So," I said. "What is it you want from me?"

Haymann unglued himself from the window and turned back to us.

"Gérard Sergent went to the police and they treated him like a dog. He has information to give, information and names. But he thinks that if he gives them to the police, it'll be pointless and they'll bury the affair."

"That's right," Sergent agreed. "Because, see, they're all in cahoots."

"Who they?" I asked.

He made a vague gesture.

"The damn immigrants," said Haymann. "Our young friend here thinks that France is in the hands of Jews and Mafiosi, that's why."

"I wouldn't go that far!" the brother exclaimed.

"So," Haymann continued without paying any attention to him, "I strongly recommended that he talk to you, a good Frenchman and a former gendarme who left the force to devote himself to the fight against scum."

I looked at him wide-eyed, but he was on a roll.

"I warned our friend that you were expensive," he said, "but he doesn't care. He understands perfectly that that's the price of incorruptibility."

"Besides, it's for my sister," Gérard added. "Money is no object when it's my sister we're talking about. Avenging my sister."

"I explained to him that you offered a flat rate. For such a revolting affair, I thought I could propose that you'd go down to 3,500 francs in advance, and the rest when you've solved the crime."

He was completely mad. I opened my mouth.

"Plus expenses," Haymann said.

"I'll write you a check immediately," said Gérard Sergent. I shut my mouth.

"Let's go down to the office," Haymann said. "Sergent will write the check, and then he'll give us the names and the information."

The young man stood up. He seemed almost enthusiastic. I stood up as well. Haymann pinched my arm. I looked at him and shrugged. I went to say goodbye to Stanislavski, and then we went downstairs.

10

WHEN GÉRARD Sergent left, Haymann stayed. As for me, I had a check for 3,500 in my pocket and I was supposed to call the brother at a hotel in the Latin Quarter as soon as I had news. I wondered what fucking news I would be able to get, and when.

The brother's theory was simple: when one of the six or seven bastards who were swarming around his sister had wanted to bang her, she put up a fight and he killed her.

"It doesn't hold water," I said out loud.

"Obviously," said Haymann.

He was leaning against the window and looking at me, blinking slowly like a contented cat.

"You're a bit of a bastard," I said.

"Why? Because I helped you siphon money off a piece of garbage?"

"He's just a kid."

"It's kids like that who joined the Milice. You're too young to remember. I, however, remember."

Given his tone of voice, I understood there was a question I shouldn't ask him just then, about him and the Milice or else him and a member of his family, or a friend. I'd ask it later. Or else never.

"What surprises me," said Haymann, "is that he doesn't seem to believe that Memphis Charles did it."

"Maybe he doesn't even know she exists."

He looked at me with an odd expression.

"What the hell were you doing all afternoon?" he asked. "Didn't you buy the paper?"

"Yes," I answered. "They're saying it could have been a burglary."

"You didn't get the latest edition," Haymann remarked calmly.

He dug his hand into his flannel jacket and from an inside pocket he pulled out a copy of the evening paper folded in eight. He tossed it onto the desk. I unfolded it. This time, Memphis Charles was on the front page.

It showed just her face and, as for the deceased Griselda, she'd been relegated to page 5, and the picture was of just her face too. MURDERED STARLET: VICTIM OF HER FRIEND? it said, and the question mark was just for show. Because the story was damning. The murder weapon belonged to the brunette (she'd bought that fucking knife in Corsica last summer, and Coquelet had already discovered its provenance; he was a smart little bugger when he wanted to be). Her fingerprints were on it—hers and no one else's. And then a bundle of bloody clothes was found in a trash bin, and of course they were hers. And to top it off, the girl was nowhere to be found. It was an open-and-shut case.

"You're making a face," Haymann said.

I had nothing to say to that.

"And they didn't even mention the acid."

"Acid?" (I was distracted, trying to think.)

"The LSD in the apartment," said Haymann. "And traces of all sorts of shit in the dead girl's blood. Believe you me, I spent my day buzzing around the cops, putting together bits and pieces of information. Our little Griselda had one hell of a cocktail in her veins, according to the autopsy. No hard stuff, but all that junk they've invented now for kids to use. Amphetamines and so on. And hashish along with strawberry jelly in her stomach."

"Enough," I said. "I'm starving. Don't spoil my appetite."

I explained that I hadn't eaten a thing since yesterday. He felt sorry for me.

"Let's go downstairs," he said. "I'll be damned if we can't find a hotdog and fries on the boulevard. We'll talk while we eat."

I shook my head. I wanted to think first.

"About what, for God's sake?"

"About everything the young guy said to me," I answered. "We have to rack our brains."

"Tarpon," Haymann said, "you're getting on my nerves. You know where Memphis Charles is. All you have to do is hand her over to the cops on a silver platter and the other little asshole will show you 3,500 more francs. Why torture yourself? She knocked off her friend. It's obvious."

"Too obvious."

Haymann took his head in his hand, comically, and he paced the office, moaning.

"Oy! Oy! Oy!" he groaned. "What kind of a cockamamie reply is that? We're not in Hollywood. When all the clues point in the same direction, it doesn't mean that the senator was a victim of a frame job, it simply means that all the clues point in the same direction."

I didn't understand the thing about the senator, but I didn't bother bringing it up.

"The fingerprints on the knife," I said. "It doesn't add up. Everyone loves playing with a knife. A Laguiole is really beautiful. It isn't normal that the girl's fingerprints were the only ones on it."

Haymann raised his arms to the sky and sat in the armchair meant for visitors. Still, he didn't reply. I could tell he was thinking.

"Maybe she kept it buried in a drawer where no one had the opportunity to see or touch it," he said at last.

"Yeah, sure," I said.

And I meant it. If I'd known where the kid was, I think I would have turned her over to the police then and there. Maybe.

"So what are we going to do?" Haymann asked, exasperated.

"We're thinking," I sighed. "We'll go down the list of names that Gérard Sergent gave us."

Haymann waved his arm in a way that signified I had a screw loose, but that he was willing to entertain my fantasies for a moment. I grabbed the piece of paper on which I'd taken notes and made little doodles while the brother was talking to me.

"Lyssenko," I read. "Over thirty. Director of *Forbidden Caresses*."

Haymann shook his head, sighing. He still seemed very grumpy and dismissive.

"Never heard of him," he huffed. "I'll have to call my friend at *France-Presse*. Next?"

"Alexis Vacher. Forty years old. Director of the two other films starring our Griselda."

"Along with *The Vampire's Hymen* and *K.G.B. Orgies*. You gotta see that last one, it's a disaster. A pornographic spy thriller. Anyway…He must have made two or three other ones. Not a killer type, in any event."

"You know him?"

"Not personally, but I've heard of him. Not a repressed sort of guy, if you get my drift."

I wasn't sure I did, but I accepted it.

We went on examining the list. Haymann said he knew most of the men well enough to put them in the harmless category. Skirt chasers, definitely; dishonest, perhaps; murderers, no. We were getting to the end of the list.

"Eddy Alfonsino."

"A small-time thug," Haymann said. "Mixed up in two or three jobs. Probably a snitch too. A pimp for sure. And I wouldn't be surprised if he was a dealer for the acid and the other stuff, but a killer, no."

The same old song. I let out a long sigh.

"That's it," I said.

"So you see. Not a single suspect in the pile. We could have saved ourselves the trouble."

I shook my head.

"Still, there are three I'm keeping in mind. Lyssenko and Vacher, first of all, the two directors. Good family men you say. Precisely."

Haymann let out a sad little laugh. In his opinion, I was as good at psychology as a horse is at navigation.

"Or as a former gendarme is for reasoning," he concluded.

"And Alfonsino," I said. "A small-time thug, okay. But I'd be curious to know if he has guts."

"You should start by putting your check in the bank."

"At this time of day," I pointed out, "it's closed. But I am going to start by chowing down. You can be my guest."

He shook his head.

"Now that I think about it," he said, "I'm grateful, but no thanks. I'd be better off digging around some more, because you won't manage by yourself at the rate you're going."

He wearily extricated himself from the armchair.

"What kept you this afternoon?" he asked.

"If I told you, you wouldn't believe me," I said.

"You were with the girl, eh? Memphis Charles, I mean."

I said I would have liked that better. And then I wrote down the license plate numbers of the Mercedes and the Toronado.

"You can check who owns these cars," I sighed.

Haymann grumbled and pocketed the piece of paper. Then he left, promising to call me. It didn't seem like he was in a good mood. I hadn't even thanked him for the 3,500 francs, I mean for helping me scoop them up. I wondered if he was expecting a commission. Then a clock chimed eight times from the drunk's apartment below me, and I crawled out of my thoughts. Night had fallen more than halfway. I left to chow down, like I'd said.

11

As I exited my building, I wasn't surprised to see Coccioli spying on me. He was sitting in a black Citroën DS, with his bandage on his face, trying to hide behind a copy of the comic magazine *Pilote*. I was just about to head over to him to ask him to drive me to the restaurant. Might as well take advantage of the fact that he was tailing me. But as I was stepping off the sidewalk to cross over to him, surprising things happened on the other side of the street.

There were quite a few people around, and nowadays you see all sorts of crazies, but this was the first time that right in front of me some crackpot was pointing a fire extinguisher at a car that wasn't burning.

The crackpot was young and bearded, wearing greenish fatigues and a narrow-brimmed safari hat. He was coming up behind Coccioli's DS, walking briskly, a red fire extinguisher under his arm, and he raised the extinguisher up high and sent a cloud of something that wasn't carbonic foam onto the car. The windows and the body of the DS became damp. A blindsided Coccioli dropped his *Pilote* and I glimpsed him making a motion as if to wipe away condensation around him. The whole thing took about three seconds. Another bearded guy, this one wearing a suit, six steps behind the first one, tossed under the car a projectile that looked like some kind of tin tube; it exploded with a popping sound.

Then the cloud of aerosol surrounding the car suddenly and completely caught fire. The car was transformed into nothing but flames. One second it was there, and the next it was totally yellow and red and leapt in the air boiling and making a purring sound. My jaw dropped.

"Get in this car, and hop to it," a voice ordered me.

At the same time, someone shoved a hard object in my back and an old bluish gray Peugeot 203 pulled up alongside of me, a door opened, and I was propelled inside.

Across the street the flames were fading as quickly as they'd burst out. A spray of smoke and sparks flew toward the sky between the buildings. The DS reappeared, smoking, its windows blackened. People were running in every direction.

I was fucking sick and tired of being taken for a ride. I didn't consider the danger and I turned around and smacked the owner of the voice on the wrist. He was an Arab wearing jeans and a threadbare duffle coat. His gun (hexagonal barrel, a Webley or something like that) fell on the sidewalk.

"Don't be stupid," said the Arab, bending foolishly to retrieve his piece. "Memphis Charles sent us."

I kicked him in the chin and he fell on the sidewalk, flat on his back. And then I was clubbed on the head. I got very angry. I turned toward the 203, my fist ready to smash a nose, and I stopped myself in midstream because I was face to face with a young woman. She took advantage of this to bop me again on the head with her Manufrance mail-order club. This time I felt the impact all the way down to my heels.

"That's enough now!" I said, slapping the madwoman of Chaillot.

Meanwhile, above the roof of the 203, I could see Coccioli disentangling himself from his DS. Opening the door must have made the air rush in or something, because the flames flared again inside the car and under the hood. Coccioli was swatting his clothing hard. People kept on running in all directions. The two bearded pyromaniacs were nowhere in sight.

I let myself fall to my knees, sensing the Arab was about to ambush me from behind. He jumped on me with sound and fury and the butt of his Webley cut through the air in the neighborhood of my nose. I rolled over onto my back on the sidewalk and threw him off. He punched like an amateur and sadly I'm no professional in that domain either. Also, my reflexes had been slowed by the great uncertainty in which I found myself. The young woman kept prancing around the two of us, striking out at random. The Arab was being hit more than I was. Luckily, Manufrance clubs are not that dangerous. They're nothing but rubber with lead weights.

Passersby were assembling around the human cluster we were forming, but they didn't dare intervene. Just when the rain of blows was winding down, I glimpsed the local butcher running toward us, meat ax in hand.

"Better let it drop," I advised my adversaries and was immediately punched.

"You're gonna get in this car," cried the Arab.

His voice had a note of hysteria in it. He was very young and didn't look like a hood. Once again he aimed his Webley at me. The barrel was rusty. If the kid fired, the weapon would probably explode. He'd lose a hand, and I'd be blind and disfigured.

So I flinched terribly when I heard a shot. But it wasn't the Webley. Twisting around on the sidewalk, I saw Coccioli, who'd decided to come running. He fired a second time in the air and his mouth produced indistinct cries. In the background of the falling night, the DS was now burning brightly.

"Careful," I said. "He's an imbecile. He's going to shoot at us."

Meanwhile, the butcher, who was running toward us, seeing Coccioli scream and strafe the sky, took a turn and jumped on him with his axe. They collided just when the young woman was clubbing me on the head again. I saw a spark fly from Coccioli's hand and felt the repercussion of the impact on the young woman's wrist. She looked at me, horrified.

"Oh, ow!" she cried as she fell on me.

I tried to prevent her head from landing on the ground. Just then, out of nowhere, the two bearded pyromaniacs joined the fray. The one who still had the red extinguisher thing smacked me hard on the bridge of my nose.

"Cut it out! Look at the results of your screwups!" I stammered in a furious voice.

Furious, but limp. I was totally limp. I felt someone pick me up under my arms and toss me inside the 203. Tears were streaming from my eyes, I've no idea why. I fell helplessly between the back seat and the back of the front seats. I could only see the dusty floor mat while people walked over me, doors slammed, and idiots honked on the street. The 203 took off in a groan of worn gears. There was another boom, either from a backfire or a gun. Something sticky and warm was dripping on my face. I tried to raise my head.

"Someone's bleeding," I said. "It's the girl. From your screwups."

I suffered another blow from the extinguisher, then a foot was placed on my cheek, holding my head down against the floor mat. It was filthy, I didn't give a damn, I was way past that now. Besides, shortly afterward the foot let up its pressure and someone put a potato sack over my head. There was still dirt at the bottom of it. I attempted to sneeze to get rid of it, but someone twisted my arms around to my back and put handcuffs on my wrists and then another pair on my ankles.

"The girl is bleeding," I repeated from inside my sack. "Put a tourniquet on her, for God's sake!"

They smacked me on the head again. My little remaining light of consciousness scurried off toward a long tunnel. I tried to catch it.

"A tourniquet?" I said again and they must have whacked me again, because the little light emitted an ironic chuckle and disappeared.

12

"YOU'RE a bunch of wackos!" said a voice I thought I recognized.

I was of exactly the same opinion. I opened my eyes. I was lying on a bed and no longer had a bag over my head, but I still had handcuffs on my wrists and ankles, and there must have been a chain tying me to the bedframe because I couldn't move; I was splayed out like a rabbit at the butcher's.

It was Memphis Charles who'd just spoken. If I hadn't been so furious, I would've confessed I was happy to see her again. She was really very pretty. She was wearing the same outfit as—holy shit—what was only the previous day, a bit soiled perhaps, and she looked dog-tired. She was arguing loudly with the Arab and one of the two pyromaniacs—the one who'd sprayed the gasoline with his giant atomizer, and who'd also clocked me.

I had a miserable headache, worse than a sinus infection, and it was keeping me from thinking. I let my eyes roam over the small room. It was badly kept and not of recent construction. The ochre wallpaper with little pink flowers was dotted with mold and fly shit and peeling at the seams. From what I could make out, the flooring was rough and soiled with plaster drippings and cigarette butts. There was a door with a coat hook screwed into it and a window. All was dark outside. Inside, a yellow bulb lit the room, the bed, a cane chair next to the bed, and a dresser from the Second Empire, I think, the kind where the drawers are always getting stuck.

"The girl," I muttered groggily. "What did you do with the injured girl?"

They immediately interrupted their argument to look at me with annoyance. If I annoyed them, they shouldn't have made me come is how I felt.

"She'll be okay," said Memphis Charles.

"A doctor," I growled.

"We've got one." (It was the Arab putting in his two cents and he was acting high and mighty.)

"Who's 'we'?"

"Don't answer him," the bearded guy said to the Arab.

The Arab just shrugged.

"We're anti-imperialists," the bearded guy said scornfully. "You wouldn't understand."

I closed my eyes. Perhaps I was going to wake up in my little bedroom and my mommy would bring me hot chocolate in bed because I'd been really sick, I was delirious, I saw things that weren't real and all that. I opened my eyes. I saw the same thing I'd seen when I shut them, except that the three preposterous persons had come closer to me and were flanking the bed, Memphis Charles on one side, the bearded guy and the Arab on the other.

"I'm not an imperialist," I said with all my common sense. "Why have you tied me up?"

"See how ridiculous this is?" cried Memphis Charles.

Should I thank her? I tried hard to slip a hand out of the handcuffs, but I only managed to hurt myself. Meanwhile, my three clowns had started yelling at each other again over my head, and the result of the discussion was that they should never have brought me here, according to Memphis Charles.

"Even if he's only being manipulated," said the bearded guy, "that doesn't mean he isn't dangerous."

"I'm going to be any minute!" I shouted. "I'm going to become very dangerous if someone doesn't get me something to eat!"

They looked at me like I was nuts. They couldn't understand, obviously. Still, I was dying of hunger.

"You'll eat if you talk," said the bearded guy.

"About what, for Pete's sake?"

"Don't play dumb," he answered. "That doesn't work with me. I know where you come from, Mr. Cop."

"Everyone does," I sighed.

"I'm not talking about Saint-Brieuc," said the bearded guy. "I'm talking about all the rest."

He had a nasty face. He scared me because you could smell his stupidity a mile away, and because he had a fiery, fanatical look in his eyes. "Industrial Support and Security," he added.

I blinked.

"Huh?"

He repeated it.

"Does that mean anything to you?" he yapped. "Does the name Foran ring a bell?"

"Uh...yeah, it does," I admitted, opening my eyes wide.

"Bastard!" cried the bearded guy and he started slapping me left and right.

I gritted my teeth. The Arab took his friend by the arm to calm him down. In fact, the Arab seemed just as surprised as I was.

"What on earth are you talking about?" he whispered in the bearded guy's ear.

"This chap," said the bearded guy pointing at my right

eye, "was in the same gendarme unit as Foran, the Nazi from the ISS. That explains a lot."

"That explains nothing," the Arab responded. "You forget that Charlotte went to him on her own. He didn't go looking for her."

"But at first he refused to help her, and then he was spotted at the murder site. He received orders in between, it's obvious!"

I would've really liked to know what the hell was going on. Just then, the door to the bedroom crashed open and the second bearded guy dashed in. He had a machine gun in his hand.

"There's a car coming down the path," he said. "The headlights are turned off."

He was gesticulating wildly to emphasize his words. I fearfully closed my eyes because he was going to seriously wound four or five people from one second to the next if he kept waving his weapon around.

"Let's get rid of this guy," said the first bearded guy as he rushed at me.

"There's no time," said the second bearded guy.

"I'm giving the orders!" said the Arab, but he didn't seem so sure about it.

Meantime, the first bearded guy took out a key and unlocked a pair of handcuffs, the ones on my hands. I tried to sit up on the bed, but my wrists collapsed under my weight and I fell back down. I had absolutely no feeling in my limbs.

The second bearded guy stomped toward the dark window and looked down into the night as black as blackberry pie.

"They've stopped!" he hissed. "They're getting out! They're coming!"

The first bearded guy took the handcuffs from my ankles

and stood me up by pulling on my tie. I fell right down onto the floor.

"You made those handcuffs too tight," I said. "I can't walk."

"Let's get the fuck out of here," cried the second bearded guy. "They're in the yard! I can't see them anymore . . . Oh, shit!"

The first bearded guy stared at me with loathing in his eyes.

"Just carry me," I suggested. "I only weigh seventy-six kilos."

"Fuck it, I'm getting the hell out of here," said the first bearded guy as he raced out of the room.

"Traitor! Bastard!" screamed the second bearded guy as he ran after the first.

We heard them tearing down the stairs. The Arab looked at me. He seemed unsure of what was going on. He didn't look like an idiot, but he didn't seem very nice either.

"Mr. Tarpon," he said, "if I were sure of what my . . . comrade was assuming, I would kill you here and now."

"I don't know what he assumes," I sighed. "I didn't understand a word of what he was saying."

There was a sound of breaking glass from downstairs, which eliminated all the Arab's hesitation. He rushed toward the door.

"See you again sometime, maybe," he said as he disappeared.

I looked at Memphis Charles, who'd just sat down on the bed. She was pale. She seemed to be more and more tired. Completely depressed too.

"You're not escaping with them?"

"I've had it up to here," she sighed.

Feeling was coming back into my hands and feet and I sat on my backside writhing in pain.

"What's the matter?"

"It stings," I explained, gritting my teeth.

I clumsily massaged my ankles. The pain increased, then suddenly decreased. Meanwhile, I was listening to the voices downstairs. I heard a door slam, twice. Now someone was coming up the stairs, someone very, very cautious. If the steps hadn't squeaked, I wouldn't have even known he was there.

"It's not the cops," I murmured, looking at the girl.

She grew wan and stood up, but before she could do anything else, a guy bounded into the bedroom and fell with his back against the wall. An amazing stunt. And he was covering the whole room with his Ruger. It was an automatic that I'd seen before, and I'd also seen the chap before. In a Toronado. In a flophouse. In the Verrières woods.

"Hello," he said, in English.

How was I supposed to respond to that?

13

HE GOT up slowly. He wasn't wearing his sunglasses, which was understandable because it was past midnight. His arm was almost stretched completely out in front of him and his wrist moved slightly and regularly, in such a way that the barrel of the Ruger was drawing circles in the air. I couldn't attribute the movement to nerves. The guy seemed about as nervous as a quart of milk.

"Don't move," he said.

Well, for my part, I couldn't. I realized that Memphis Charles was tense; I could practically see her muscles quivering beneath her leather jacket.

"Do what he says, honey," I advised.

Pappy Ruger squinted at the girl.

"Who's she?" he asked. "Is she Charlotte Schultz? Yes? No?"

It took me a second to remember that Charlotte Schultz was the girl's real name. I nodded.

"We wait," said the gunman.

We waited. I recovered all the feeling in my hands and feet.

"Just what are we waiting for?" I asked then.

He didn't answer. I would have liked to disarm him. In all the books, a professional gunman is easily disarmed. Someone shoots at the rug and he falls down like a fool, or else someone whacks him on the head with a bedside lamp, or else someone discreetly slips the refill for a gas cigarette lighter into the fireplace, it explodes after a minute or two, and the bad guy is knocked out by the explosion. Well, in this fucking bedroom there was neither rug nor lamp, nor fireplace (nor refill for a lighter), nothing except the furniture and the four walls. I moved imperceptibly on my rear end toward the cane chair. Pappy Ruger made a reproachful sound with his mouth.

"You don't move, I said."

I stopped moving. Maybe I could take off a shoe and throw it at the lightbulb. But my shoes have laces; I'm not a beatnik. When I surreptitiously started to undo a knot, Pappy Ruger made his mouth noise again.

"Tarpon," he said. "Stop your antics."

I stopped.

Just then, the guy's wingman came into the room, a lot more normally than his friend had. He was carrying bearded guy number two's machine gun under his arm, and he had a Mauser HSc in his hand that I recognized because it's a very elegant, quick, and attractive weapon. And it makes very, very big holes.

The two guys started speaking to each other animatedly in their language, not at all coldly the way you'd expect two killers to speak.

"By any chance do you understand what they're saying?" I asked the girl, without much hope.

She nodded. She seemed distraught.

"They caught my... my friends. At the back door. They're locked in downstairs."

"Alive?" I asked.

At this point, I figured anything could happen.

"For now, it would seem."

"Are they speaking English?"

"American. And they're really obscene. Happy now?"

"I'm just trying to keep up," I said, "that's all."

The man with the Mauser placed the machine gun along the wall and sat against said wall to cover us with his revolver. Pappy Ruger approached us, looking over his shoulder to make sure he didn't get in his friend's line of fire.

"You don't move," he said. "I search you."

He did what he said. Once again he took my keys, my watch, and my ballpoint pen, and from Memphis Charles he took some beauty things, like a nail file, along with her wallet.

"You don't move," he said again (it must have been the fourth or fifth time).

He and his acolyte walked out of the room backwards and shut the door. I heard the key turning in the lock. Memphis and I stayed motionless for a few seconds listening to them go down the stairs. Then she ran over to the window and opened it.

"Let me do that," I shouted, getting clumsily to my feet.

She stood still but it wasn't because of me. She shut the window.

"There's a third guy downstairs," she said.

I went to look out the window. I could vaguely make out a shape having a cigarette near the front steps. I supposed it was the Toronado driver. He was too far away for me to jump on his head with my two feet.

I looked at the surroundings to try to get an idea of the décor. We were on the second floor of an isolated house somewhere in the boonies. Thanks to the light in the bedroom, I could make out a kind of rundown garden. But beyond that, everything was completely dark except for one or two lights one or two good kilometers away. Only once did headlights illuminate the horizon, the curve of a hill five or six kilometers away as the crow flies.

"Where are we?" I asked.

"In the Val d'Oise region. Near Magny-en-Vexin."

I turned toward the girl.

"You wanted to see me?"

"Huh?"

It was a question asked with bewilderment, but not at all negatively.

"You must be a leftist," I said. "Or else Griselda Zapata was, but I think it's you. So. Someone killed Griselda. You ask for my help and I refuse to give it to you. So. You go looking for help somewhere else. From your friends. So."

"Stop saying 'So'!" she screamed.

"Fine. Therefore you went to hide at your friends'. And after a while, you sent them to get me. Which means you must have something new to tell me."

"Uhhh..." said the girl, shaking her head with annoyance, but not negatively, and her hair swayed back and forth.

"And I'd add," I added, "that your friends are totally nuts. They really didn't need to set up a crazy commando operation to get me. Are you sure the wounded girl will be okay?"

Memphis Charles stopped wriggling and leaned against the wall. She had rings under her eyes. She nodded but without much confidence.

"I...I think so," she said. "I didn't see...the wounded girl. They didn't bring her here, but the bullet came out, at least that's what they told me; it only pierced the flesh on her hip, without touching the bone. They're able to...I mean, they're organized well enough to take care of her."

"Still, what a waste," I said.

I noticed my hands were shaking, either from anger or hunger.

"You're the waste," the young girl shouted. "If you'd agreed to help me from the start, we wouldn't be here now!"

I wondered where we would be. Both in jail most likely. I sighed. What was the point in arguing? I sat down on the edge of the bed.

"What did they mean by that stuff about manipulation?" I asked. "What does the ex-gendarme Foran have to do with all that?"

"Nothing, nothing."

"Nothing?" I shouted.

"Would you have a cigarette?" she asked.

"No."

"You are annoying."

That was a good one. But I didn't respond, and she couldn't light up but she went on talking.

"You know," she said, "it's not like I was doing what I wanted here. I was practically a prisoner. Those three guys, and the girl you saw and who was wounded, were my friends, yeah, but I didn't really know them well."

"Yet you went to hide at their place."

"Well, I came to see you, didn't I? And I hardly knew you."

This is true, I thought. I groaned.

"Go on."

"They're the only guys I know who have some experience hiding out. They're ultra-far-left-wing, you know."

The fact is that their leftness went a bit *too* far. But I didn't want to argue. It was already complicated enough.

"I know," I said. "The Molotov cocktails in the basement belong to them, right?"

"I was just doing them a favor."

Now *she* was disarming, if I can express it that way.

"Anyway," she continued, "when I left your place, I went over to theirs. Except I had to spice up the story a little so they would help me. I'll spare you the details."

"No you won't," I said. "Don't spare me. Spice it up? With what exactly?"

She started wriggling nervously again and waving her hair around.

"Um . . . I hinted that maybe it was me they were after and not Griselda, that maybe she'd been killed by mistake, that maybe it was something political. Don't look at me like that!"

"How do you want me to look at you?"

"You're looking at me the way my father did when he thought I'd messed up."

"I'm not your father."

"But you think I messed up."

"Don't you?"

She started pacing back and forth. She asked me again if I had a cigarette, and I told her I still didn't.

"I couldn't predict what would happen," she said. "They're so dramatic. They spend their nights talking about terrorism, they don't dare use the phone because they think all phones are tapped, and they created a whole novel out of what I told them."

She turned to face me and made that bizarre movement I'd already seen the other evening, nodding her head up then down. It was probably simply to toss her hair away from her face, but it looked like she was drowning, trying to keep her head above water.

"Is it true you were in the same gendarme unit as Charles Foran?" she asked.

"Yes. Why?"

"You know that that guy sets up employer militias?"

"I found out," I said.

I didn't tell her I'd just found out the day before, straight out of Foran's mouth. She would have hit the ceiling.

"And something like that," I said, "is enough for your little friends to imagine I'm some sort of informant? Why not an Israeli spy while we're at it?"

"Oh!" Memphis Charles murmured. "They thought about that..."

She came to sit next to me on the bed.

"I'm going to turn myself in to the cops," she said in a weary voice. "I wanted... I'd only been here a couple of hours when I realized I wanted all this to end, for them to stop their nonsense, and to turn myself in. But my... friends would never have let me do that. Because I knew their hideout here and they were convinced I was at the center of a horrible political assassination plot, because that's what I'd led them to believe. Oh, fuck, what an asshole I am!"

"Don't be so hard on yourself," I said, somewhat distractedly. "It's pointless. And it doesn't explain why I was nabbed in the middle of the street."

"I wanted you to come. I thought the two of us could find a way out of here."

"How nice of you to have put me in the shit. All by your lonesome you'd never have been able to leave. Just who did you think would believe that?"

"For fuck's sake!" she shouted. "Can't you get it through your head? They live in a dream world. They were sure I'd be killed if I turned myself in. They wanted to protect me, even against myself."

I shook my head to try to get my thoughts in line. I don't

know if it was because of lack of food or lack of sleep, but living in a dream was becoming my main activity. And the reality of the situation wasn't doing anything to help. Obviously Memphis Charles's story didn't hold water, but what does these days? Twenty-year-old kids attacking police stations with bottles of gasoline? And I'd killed a kid, who was merely throwing paving stones, with a grenade to his face. The world is crazy. I should have gone back to Mom's like I'd planned.

"Why didn't your friends simply come to get me?" I groaned.

"There was a cop on a stakeout in front of your place. They had to take him out."

"Had to!" I repeated.

"Anyway," said Memphis Charles, "even if they were nuts to begin with, in the end they were right. It's like magic," she added ambiguously. "It always works in the end. You dance to make it rain and sooner or later it rains."

"Rains?" I repeated. I was completely lost.

"Those guys who came in right before?" said Memphis Charles. "They're Israeli agents. Obviously."

14

WHEN PAPPY Ruger opened the door again, I still hadn't recovered. Craziness is catching. I was making up theories in my head: Was Haymann an Israeli agent? And was it in fact Memphis Charles they'd tried to assassinate the other night? My theories were collapsing one by one, but I started constructing them all over again. At the same time, I was dreaming of steak frites. And it was getting mixed up in my theories. Béarnaise sauce was dripping down the faces of Palestinians. In my head, I mean. In my head.

"You come with us," said Pappy Ruger.

I asked where to. He shook his head, smiling.

"Another conversation with the crying man?" I asked.

He shrugged. I took Memphis Charles by the arm. It was nice to touch her. She was trembling nervously.

"They're going to bury us in the yard," she stated.

"Shut up," I said. "You're not letting me think."

Pappy Ruger's automatic pivoted while we went out. His friend, the guy with the Mauser, was waiting for us on the landing. If I'd really thought they were going to kill us, I would have done something crazy right then. But I thought I'd gone mad only to a point. I went down the stairs in a disciplined way, still holding the girl by the arm. The gun-toters walked down behind us.

The stairway ended in a short hallway. At one end, an

opaque door (back door, I thought); at the other end, the front door with its frosted panes. The long foyer, with two closed side doors. They shoved us toward the front door, and I don't know how things would have gone if I'd let them run their course. What happened next was that I heard an animal's groan in the foyer, like a wounded rabbit. It was coming from one of the two closed doors, and we were level with it. I didn't think. I opened a door.

The room had no windows. Lit by a bulb in a cage on the ceiling, it was some kind of workshop, with exposed pipes. The two bearded guys were attached to the pipes and they were as white as sheets. The Arab was attached to a workbench. He had one hand in a vise, and he was the one moaning like a wounded rabbit. His fingers were black and red.

I had let go of Memphis Charles. I turned around in the doorway. Pappy Ruger had grabbed the girl and was backing up, holding her tightly against him so she couldn't move. His teammate was taking his charming Mauser out of his pocket. Half my body was inside the workshop, and a tool rack against one of the walls was in my field of vision to my right. I wasn't aware of what I was doing because my arm worked faster than my brain. All I saw was my fist coming down with a hammer in it on Mauser Man's wrist.

I broke his forearm. He let out a kind of growl, a cry of pain and rage, restrained behind gritted teeth, and I rushed at him with all my weight, holding the hammer in front of me like a battering ram. He fell on his back and his skull resounded against the floor. The Mauser had fallen to the ground.

At the same time, Pappy Ruger was trying to aim his weapon at me, but Memphis Charles was holding on to his arm and she scratched him and bit his hand like an animal, screaming obscenities that I'd never heard from the mouth of a young woman, even though I lived in a rough neighborhood. The gunman was swearing as well, and he punched the girl on the head. Just then, I struck him with my hammer and he collapsed. In the workshop, the two bearded guys were screaming for help. Good thing the house was in a secluded spot.

I grabbed Memphis Charles, who was dizzy from the punch, and she scratched my hand. I dragged her back inside the workshop. On the way, I struck Mauser Man again on the head as he was trying to stand up, and then, as the front door was opening, I threw the hammer at the frosted windowpanes and picked up the Mauser. Through the breaking glass, I saw the Toronado driver holding a Colt and looking surprised.

"Don't move or I'll shoot," I yelled like an idiot, and he shot at me.

It wasn't a .22. The noise was so terrifying that I closed my eyes and pressed the trigger, aiming haphazardly. I opened my eyes and the driver had disappeared. I was in the doorway to the workshop and had one knee on the ground. I didn't remember kneeling. Otherwise, I felt like I was in one piece.

I glanced over my shoulder. Pappy Ruger wasn't where I'd left him either. He must've been starting to sit up when the driver shot. The bullet from the Colt had hit him in the head, and the impact had propelled his body some two or three meters backwards. He was now at the foot of the stairs with his head, or what was left of it, on the first step. I wondered if, while he was alive, he was just as bad a driver as the driver was a shooter.

"Wha…wha…what happened?" asked Memphis Charles. Her teeth were chattering. She was curled up against the workshop wall, her legs under her chin and her hands on her ears. The foyer smelled of cordite.

"Shhh," I said, examining the front door.

On the lower, wooden part, smack in the middle, I found the impact of my own bullet. A .32 ACP is supposed to be able to plow through a door without too much difficulty. I got a bad taste in my mouth, a bad taste that I recognized, and I took the risk of crawling up to the door, hooking the wood part with one finger, and pulling it toward me, ready for another exchange of gunfire.

There wasn't one. There was no need. The driver was stretched out on his back in front of the entrance, a dark stain the size of a plate in the middle of his chest, and it was spreading. The hall light was reflected in the man's open eyes. Once again I had killed someone, and once again I didn't know why. I thought I was going to be sick. I brought my left hand to my mouth and bit my knuckles. I gagged a couple of times, but things calmed down without getting worse.

I stood up, weary, letting the Mauser hang from my hand. I went back into the workshop. I wanted to deal with the Arab, but Memphis Charles had loosened the vise and pulled out his hand. She hadn't done anything else. The two bearded guys, suspended from the pipes like owls on an attic door, were braying like asses.

"Untie us! Are you going to untie us, you bastard?"

"Should I?" I asked the girl.

I was undecided. I looked at the Arab who was still attached to the workbench and who had placed his injured hand in front of him. He was blowing on it. He had three broken fingers. He must have been suffering quite a bit.

"Why did they do that to you?" I asked.

"They wanted to know who we were, what we had to do with you and Memphis. And with Griselda Zapata."

"And you told them?"

He sniffled scornfully and pointed to the two bearded guys with his chin.

"They talked. Without anyone laying a hand on them."

I sighed.

"I'd love to have the time to convince you that all of this shit has nothing to do with Palestine..."

"I already figured that out," said the Arab, interrupting me. "The way they asked questions. And the questions themselves. I got it."

"I see," I said. "So. Is your Peugeot parked around here?"

"In the garage. Under the house."

"Your hand is screwed too. You need to see a doctor. I'll free you. Take your car and get out of here. I don't want to know where you go. I never want to hear a word about any of you again. Do we agree?"

"Yes."

"Better late than never," I mumbled and freed them, and they gave my Mauser and me a nasty glance, but they didn't cause any trouble and they left in their Peugeot.

I went back into the house. Memphis Charles had dragged the American who was still alive into the workshop and she was attaching him to the pipes. Life goes on, like the song says. I retied her poorly tied knots and then searched the guy as he was coming to. Not much in his pockets. Mainly credit cards in the name of Louis Caruso and an American passport with the same name and an address in some town in New Jersey.

He looked at me in silence while I was exploring. I left the workshop to go search the two corpses. The first thing

I found was a pair of gloves in the driver's pocket and I put on the darn things to keep searching without leaving my prints everywhere. It wouldn't have helped in a thorough investigation, obviously, but who can afford a thorough investigation these days?

The driver's name was Patrick Ford and the guy with the Ruger was Edward Carbone. Same stuff as the survivor: passports, credit cards, address in New Jersey, same town. A little French dough, which I took. Along with Memphis Charles's stuff (nail file, ID, etc.) and mine (watch, pen, etc.). Nothing else. No address books or anything like that, just two extra cartridges in the pocket of the guy called Carbone. I took them too, along with his Ruger. I removed the gloves and put them on him. Very unpleasant. It made me sweat.

Next I wiped the Mauser as carefully as I could and placed it in the gloved hand of the dearly departed Carbone. I told Memphis Charles not to panic, and I grabbed the corpse's arm and worked his fingers. The gun fired and the bullet lodged in the ceiling. The pistol fell on the ground but it didn't matter anymore, traces of gunpowder must have remained on the glove for their stupid tests.

I kept moving around to wipe off whatever could be wiped off, the hammer, various spots where I remembered having placed my fingers. I was sure I was forgetting some and that depressed me. Caruso looked as dead as possible. The girl was leaning on the workbench massaging her temples.

"Ask him who he works for," I said.

"I understand," Caruso interrupted, and he added some things in American.

"He says," the girl translated, "that you can do whatever you want to him, his boss would do worse things if he answered you, so he's not talking."

I sighed. I glanced at the vise. Yeah, no doubt worse things could be done. I'd had enough of this ridiculous violence. I went over to Caruso and slapped him back and forth.

"Bastard," I said with sadness in my voice. "Damn fucking bastard."

He snickered. I took a file from the tool rack and slid it between his fingers. He tensed.

"Don't worry," I said. "Hold it. It's so you can untie yourself once we're gone. And then get the fuck out of here. Understand?"

He stared at me wide-eyed, but his fingers closed over the file.

"Come on," I said to the girl. "We'll let him figure it out. Let's scram."

We scrammed.

15

WE TOOK the Toronado that was waiting on the muddy path, a short distance from the garden that had gone to seed. The driver had had the keys on him, and now I had them.

I asked the girl what she'd done with her car and she told me she'd left it in a parking lot before getting in touch with her fun pals. She didn't say where. I didn't push the matter.

I started the car in a hurry because I had no desire to hang around. Far away or not, the neighbors were going to wind up calling the emergency services, the three individuals dying to free Palestine could get it in their heads to come back here, and God knows what else. The Toronado went down the dirt path and then we came to a local road. I asked Memphis if she knew where we were. She did. She directed me. I was driving clumsily because the automatic gearbox confused me. Nevertheless, we managed to find ourselves on Highway 14 and I headed toward Pontoise and Paris.

What interested Memphis Charles the most in the car was the pack of Marlboros and the cigarette lighter she found, the former in the glove compartment, the latter on the dashboard. She quickly lit up and made as if to pass the cigarette to me. I said smoking causes cancer and she didn't insist. She didn't even laugh in my face; she must really have been down in the dumps.

What interested me the most was the radiotelephone in

the armrest. I was waiting for it to ring. It didn't ring, and the kilometers flew by. The road was almost empty. We passed a few trucks and saw a few more dotting the side of the road here and there in the night.

I turned on the radio to try to get some news and came across a frightening cacophony. I wanted to change stations but the girl told me to leave it, that it was Chick Corya or Gorya, who knows, on the synthesizer, so I left it but that did nothing to calm my nerves.

"When we get to Paris," I said when Mr. Chick had finished synthesizing chaos, "we're going straight to the police, right? You sure?"

"What else can I do?"

"I don't know. I don't like it. You shouldn't have hightailed it in the first place."

"You know I won't implicate you," she said. "I'll tell them I made a mistake."

"The other night, when I was drunk, you told me you had a motive."

"Let's not bring it up."

"Yes, let's. Did you have a motive to kill Griselda Zapata?"

She lit a third cigarette with the butt of the second.

"The little bitch stole a good role from me in *Daddy Longdick*. Okay, it's just a little crime story, but Borniol-Vilmorin is directing it. Well, I guess now he's going to have to find someone else for the part."

By the time she explained to me that *Daddy Longdick* was a book and that Borniol-Vilmorin was a director who was about to explode on the scene (I startled), we'd arrived at a roadside bar. I almost totaled the car because there's no engine braking on an automatic; nevertheless, I managed to glide the Toronado into the gravel parking lot, between the hedge and a Fruehauf trailer as big as a house. From the street, the car couldn't be seen.

"What are you doing?" the girl asked.

"I'm going to eat an entire ox if they have one," I said, and I got out of the Toronado.

They didn't have an entire ox. I consoled myself with four stale sandwiches, two Carlsbergs, a slice of fruitcake, and three cups of coffee. From time to time truck drivers would come in, order an espresso, listen to Mozart arranged for accordion and choir on the jukebox, and leave. The local drunk was sitting at one end of the counter.

"Youth!" he cried. "If it comes to get me, I won't give it any advice. I'll give it a knife. A knife!" he repeated at the top of his lungs, waving his fist.

"That's enough, Gallibet," the owner said from behind the bar.

Gallibet continued his grumbling, but his words grew less distinct. Meanwhile, the girl and I were sitting at a Formica table under a bawdy calendar distributed by the Champion candle company, and I was still stuffing myself full, she was drinking a glass of milk, and we were whispering.

"That's not a motive," I said.

"You don't get it. Griselda would have killed to get out of porn and into something else."

"But you didn't need that."

"Me? Sadly, I'm a stunt girl. And because there are only two or three stunt girls in Paris, I get lots of work, sure, but I'm always the motorcycle murderer who drives off the side of the road or else I'm the star's double in a car accident. That's not a career."

"You want a career?"

"Listen, Tarpon," she said. "I left home at sixteen. I was

starving. Now I eat but I don't know if I'll still be eating next month. It's not a life. I want dough."

"Do you think the cops will believe that's a motive?"

"I have no idea and I don't give a damn. I don't have a choice, do I? If I don't go to the cops, where will I go?"

I finished my third cup of coffee.

"You could check into a good hotel and wait a couple of days," I said. "Just enough time for me to bone up on the question. There are a few things I'd like to clear up, and you might not need to go to the police afterwards."

She looked at me. She was on her sixth cigarette in thirty-five minutes. She asked me if I thought I was Sam Spade, and once again she had to explain to me that he was a character in a novel.

"I'm in the hands of a provincial ex-gendarme who is a total philistine," she commented.

"If you'd rather be in the hands of the cops..."

"Every hotel owner is a police informant," she interrupted, pedantically. "As soon as I went out somewhere, the guy would be on the phone mobilizing law enforcement."

"You're an actress," I said. "Looking like someone else is your job."

She thought for a moment. She moved her tongue across her lip. A lovely lip. Suddenly, she didn't seem tired anymore. She seemed excited.

"Let's go back to the car," she said.

I paid with the dead guy's money and we went back to the car. The girl hopped in the back seat and got out her makeup stuff, everything the late Carbone had taken and that I'd retrieved from his body.

"Don't peek," she ordered. "I want you to see the end result and tell me if it shocks you."

I sat back in my seat. I played with the radiotelephone. It still wasn't ringing. There was a flat box next to the instrument, with a series of buttons and a lined index card slid beneath a plastic sheet. The whole thing was laid out so that each button corresponded to a line on the index card. I got a sudden impulse. I picked up the phone, listened to a strange dial tone, and pushed the first button.

The dial started to spin by itself. I hung up immediately. The spinning stopped. I smiled for the first time in a while. I took the notecard out and picked up a minuscule gold ballpoint attached to the side of the radiophone. Then I picked up the receiver and pressed the first button. The dial began to spin and I began to write. When I heard ringing on the other end of the nonexistent line, I'd written down seven numbers.

I let the phone ring for a long time, but no one answered. I hung up, then picked up the receiver again and began the routine with the second button on the gadget. I wrote down the second number. This time, someone answered. More precisely, the receiver began to broadcast a Strauss waltz in my ear, and a young woman's perverse, prerecorded voice told me over Strauss to hold the line, to be patient, that I had reached the Hilton. Okay. I had nothing to say to reception at the Hilton. I hung up and started again with the third button. Nothing happened. The dial didn't budge. Same for the other buttons (there were six in all). Four were worthless. One gave me the Hilton. One gave me a number that no one answered. Let's say that one was the number of the Mercedes. Let's say that the crying man was staying at the Hilton. It made sense. I turned back toward Memphis Charles to tell her I was pleased with myself, if not the reasons for my satisfaction, and nothing came out of my mouth.

"Good God," I said after a moment.

"Really?" she asked, and I had another shock because her voice had changed too. It was the squeaky voice of a prudish old maid.

"Your clothes don't go with *that* at all," I stated.

"They'll have to do for tonight."

True enough. She climbed back into the front seat to sit next to me. I started the car. I couldn't help throwing sideways glances her way. She had a bun and looked nearsighted. She had completely destroyed her eyelashes and redrawn her eyebrows. Her mouth had nothing sensuous about it anymore. And her posture was awful. Her shoulders were stiff but her lower back slumped and her belly poked out. Her face was slightly shiny. She looked ugly, and knowing that in reality she wasn't had a strange effect on me, some kind of tingling in my neck and along my ribs.

"Wait until tomorrow," she said. "You ain't seen nothing yet."

We bypassed Pontoise and sped toward Paris. We were on the ring road before 3:00 a.m. and at 3:15 I parked the Toronado on a street in the suburb of Montrouge. When I got out of the car, I looked at the license plate. It wasn't the same as the day before.

We walked to the Porte d'Orléans. On the way, I tossed the late Carbone's Ruger into a storm drain. A taxi took us to Montparnasse. We continued south on foot via rue René Mouchotte. In the rather seedy neighborhood that stretches out at the end of that street and that's in the process of, or destined for, demolition because of the construction of the new stretch of rue Vercingétorix, I found the kind of hotel I was looking for, not quite decent but not a total dive. I stopped ten meters from the entrance.

"I have to go up with you," I said. "It'll seem more natural since you don't have any luggage. Besides, I could use a wash. And the cops are probably waiting at my place, seeing as I was kidnapped in a sense."

She nodded without a peep.

"I hope you're not imagining anything else," I added.

She didn't laugh in my face. How sweet of her.

She simply said okay and started walking again. We went into the hotel where a grumpy, alcoholic night watchman barely looked at us as he gave us a key and cards to fill out.

There was no way to take a bath at that hour, but at least the room had a shower. Everything else about it was sordid. Memphis Charles let herself fall onto the bed.

"Geez! I'm wiped," she stated.

"Go to sleep," I said. "I'll take my shower and leave. I'll call you tomorrow at noon, I mean, today at noon."

"Hmm."

I was already behind the curtain. I hung my clothes on the edge of the stall and showered. There was no soap, but I scrubbed myself for a long time. I was trying to think. I dried myself off, badly, and put my dirty clothes back on. I left the shower. I still had a few questions to ask the kid, but she'd fallen asleep with her clothes on exactly where she'd collapsed, in the middle of a double bed. I said to myself I had nowhere to go. If I went to Haymann's, I'd have to explain myself for hours, and I'd had enough, I needed to sleep. I pushed the kid to one side and she grumbled a bit but didn't wake up. I covered her with the quilt. Before I got into bed, I took the time to wash my shirt and socks.

16

HAYMANN picked up the phone on the sixth ring.

"You bonehead halfwit!" he shouted when he recognized my voice. "What time is it?"

"Ten in the morning."

"Thanks to you, I spent the night in a daze with those gentlemen! Your place is crawling with cops. Where'd you go? They kidnapped you in a car? What is this crap?"

I said I'd tell him everything. I asked if I could hide a car in his backyard.

"Hide it in my yard? What do you mean? Bury it? Are you drunk?"

"No, I mean put it in your yard," I sighed. "Hide it behind the house."

"A stolen car?"

"Among other things."

"Among other things!" he repeated, exasperated. "Fine. Come over, Tarpon. But try to tell me some amusing stories or else this is the last favor I'll ever do for you."

I promised to try and I hung up. I walked out of the phone booth and into the subway station. I bought *Le Parisien Libéré*, and a subway took me toward Porte d'Orléans. In the paper there was a picture of me from back when I was a gendarme and where I looked ashamed. Not at all like myself. The article talked about my blood-spattered kidnapping that had wounded one Officer Coccioli, who'd suffered contusions and slight burns. A butcher had been arrested then released. According to the paper, the kidnapping might have been the revenge of left-wingers. My attackers, apparently, seemed to be North African, and everyone knew that in Saint-Brieuc, I had... In sum, the conclusion was that my kidnappers might be Maoist subproletarians hungry to carry out their own kind of justice. Not a word linking my misadventures to the Griselda Zapata affair. Something wasn't right. Not only had the police said nothing, but on top of it all, it appeared they were demanding silence on the matter. I couldn't see why.

From Porte d'Orléans, I walked. I found the Toronado where I'd left it and looked around. I was more or less expecting to see hordes of cops hiding in every corner. But there was nothing. I got into the car and took off without a hitch. Fifteen minutes later, without getting too lost, I reached Clamart and stopped in front of Haymann's place.

He was waiting for me in his little yard, his cap on his head and a scarf over his sweater with its leather elbow patches. I almost took off half the fence when I tried to pull the Toronado onto the property and drive around the house. I wound up in the vegetable garden.

"Good job," Haymann said. "Crush my lettuce, see if I care."

I opened the car door and realized that he wasn't really furious but he did a good imitation of fury. Still, he offered me a cup of coffee.

"Thanks," I said. "But I'd like us to drink it in the car, because I'm waiting for a call on this thing."

I tapped the radiotelephone in the open armrest.

"From who?" Haymann asked.

"Maybe I'll find out when I get the call."

He pouted and went in to get the java. He came back very quickly and sat down next to me with the coffeepot, two plastic mugs, a sugar bowl, and a single spoon all piled up and precariously balanced. We had our little garden party on the front seat. We drank. The coffee was burning hot; it felt good. Through the windshield we had a view of the sloping vegetable garden; it was leafy green, cheerful, and we could see the roofs of the houses beyond it, and the fumes in the valley, and apartment buildings being constructed. The weather was iffy, but there were a few rays of sun.

I told Haymann as much as I could tell him, that is, just about everything, except that in my version the two gunmen had shot each other when they were trying to get me.

"Who do you think will believe that, Tarpon?"

"You, for starters."

He tossed his cap on the car floor, let out a nasty sigh, and punched his head several times.

"Calm down," I said.

"It's okay, I'm calm," he answered, picking up his cap and twisting it back on his head. "What do you propose to do now?"

I told him that depended on where I stood under criminal law, and he explained he had gone back to my place around eleven the previous night to have a drink and tell me that the license plate numbers I'd taken down were bogus. One belonged to a school bus and the other was unassigned. In any case, when he arrived at my place, the cops who were waiting there had collared him, and Coccioli had grilled him for six hours.

"With breaks every now and then," he added. "Still, it wasn't fun. I knew you weren't straight with me about your contacts with Memphis Charles, and I wondered if I shouldn't have told them everything I knew. For your own good, Tarpon."

"Yeah, yeah," I grumbled.

"They wanted to know what I was doing at your place, and I told them we'd met last year because I'd had the idea of writing an article about you after the Saint-Brieuc business. Basically, I said I was trying to do you a favor and I'd brought Gérard Sergent to you. Since I'd been seen with him at the morgue, they would have made the connection eventually. They asked me why I had come back to see you so late at night, and what I knew about the Louise Sergent case. I said I knew less than they did, and in the end I admitted that I'd come over to get a little cut of that business since I'd brought you Gérard."

I almost asked Haymann if that was true, but something in his look stopped me. He concluded: "I looked really ashamed and that made them laugh and they let me go like the old lout that I am. It didn't cheer me up to play that part. I'd like to believe that it served some decent purpose."

"Come on," I said. "We are defending the weak and the oppressed, widows and orphans."

"Granted, Sergent lost his father," said Haymann, "but Memphis Charles is not a widow. And I'm not sure either that there's anything defensible about her. In which hotel did you leave her?"

"Why wouldn't she be defensible?" I asked instead of answering his question.

Haymann lit his cigarette for the fourth time; it kept going out.

"Last night," he said, "there was an interrogation, but there was also a conversation. The cops know me. They don't rough me up much and they chat with me. I learned some things."

"Stop fooling around then and tell me what you know."

"Griselda Zapata was not raped. But a rape was faked. In other words, she'd been penetrated, but we don't know with what, and there was no sperm."

He was speaking callously. Trying to prove he was a hard-ass.

"So, the moral of the story is that . . ."

"It could have been the work of a woman," I said, finishing his sentence.

Haymann shrugged.

"Listen," I said. "Let's wait twenty-four hours. I want to see what I can dig up about Griselda's little friends, the names her brother gave us. And then there's the crying man."

"That doesn't connect to anything. Totally incomprehensible. You sure you didn't make that up?"

"What do you take me for?"

"A fucking liar. But you don't have enough imagination to concoct a story like that out of whole cloth. So what do you intend to do now?"

"That depends if you can help me," I said. "If you can stay here and answer the phone in the car when they call."

"If they call . . ."

Now it was my turn to shrug.

"Okay, Tarpon," he sighed. "And what should I say if they call?"

"That I want to see them. I'll go over to the Hilton this evening. They should leave a message for me at reception."

He nodded. He stayed quiet for a moment, then said, "You'll waste time if you go on foot. While I'm stuck here like an idiot, you might as well take my Aronde."

17

As i was driving toward Porte de Vanves, what Haymann said to me was rattling around my brain. I mean, about Memphis Charles. In the end, instead of turning toward the east of Paris as I'd intended, I headed straight for Montparnasse. I was driving the Aronde somewhat hesitantly because I'm not in the habit of driving and because the Toronado had messed with my reflexes. It was not a good time to get into an accident, what with my name all over the papers.

I had a hard time finding a place to park. It was eleven thirty when I walked into the hotel. Given the face I was wearing on the picture in the papers, the receptionist didn't have much chance of recognizing me. Still, he called to me as I was walking in front of his desk and my heart skipped a beat.

"Your key," he said, proffering the object in question.

"My wife went out?"

"Yeah."

"Did she leave a message for me?"

"No."

When I'd gone out, I'd left Memphis Charles asleep and a note on the pillow. There was no Memphis and no note. The bed was made, the window open, and the room looked even dingier like that. It was as empty as could be. Nothing to remind anyone that the little brat had been there. She really conned me. At least that's what I was thinking, and then the door opened behind me, and I turned around and gazed with hostile surprise at the ugly stranger walking in.

"What is it?" I asked, annoyed. And then I recognized her. "Good God," I said. "I forgot you'd made yourself up like that. It's crazy when you know how pretty you are in real life."

I don't know what got into me to add that last bit. I guess I was completely caught off guard because a moment before I'd been convinced she'd cleared off.

She said thanks in a shaky voice and placed some parcels on the bed. Her movements were slightly jerky. She was wearing glasses and, with a flick of her finger, they dropped down her nose and she stared at me over the large frames.

"They're real lenses," she explained. "I pinched them from some lady's purse at the department store. She must be really nearsighted. I keep bumping into things."

"Great," I said. "Pickpocket on top of everything else."

"At least they completely fuck up my face, don't you think?"

"I don't know," I sighed. "I like women with glasses because they scare me less than the others. It's more the rest that disfigures you. The bun and all. How do you do that?"

"Trade secret," she said as she started undoing her parcels.

She'd bought clothes. A blue coarse linen skirt and a horrible red short-sleeved knit top. She spread them out on the bed.

"With these, I'll really look like a hick," she said contentedly. "Where'd you go? Your picture is in *France-Soir*. A bad picture. You're incredibly ugly in *France-Soir*. I bought you a pair of pajamas."

She took the newspaper and the pajamas in question from

a plastic bag and tossed them to the end of the bed. I must have looked bewildered because she burst out laughing.

"I woke up once at dawn," she explained. "I was shocked to see a naked man in my bed, with me on top of the blanket."

"Not naked. In my briefs."

"I didn't check. Did you know that you're quite acceptable naked? Why do you dress like a freak?"

I grumbled indignantly.

"You can keep the pajamas," I said. "I won't spend another night here."

"But you're on the lam, in a sense," she remarked.

"Spare me your literary jargon. I'm on the lam until midnight tonight. After that I'm going to the cops."

She persisted.

"At the moment, I'm your client. In fact, I'm going to write you a check. You're not going to turn your client over to the cops."

"You must have read that somewhere again," I sighed. "I don't want your check. You're not my client. And in any case, I do whatever I want."

She looked at me for a moment with an inscrutable gaze. Then she did something unexpected: she giggled. Thirty seconds later, her laughter took on worrisome proportions. She was doubled over from it. Her glasses were fogging up. She let herself fall on the bed, hiccupping constantly. I frowned. Slowly she calmed down.

"He does whatever he wants!" she panted. "He says he does whatever he wants!"

"Good God," I said. "Are you high or what?"

"He does whatever he wants!" she repeated and again started to laugh but broke off suddenly. "What did you say?" she asked, in a completely different voice.

I repeated what I'd said. She took off her glasses and wiped her eyes. Her gaze was now glacial. She shook her head.

"No, I'm not high," she said. "So. The interrogation is starting again?"

I nodded.

"I thought we were friends," she sighed.

I didn't know what to say. I sat down on the sole chair, next to the bed. And then I questioned her. She answered me in a sullen, almost distracted voice. Once again we "replayed the events," as they say in the papers. She didn't budge a millimeter in her statements.

Monday, that is, the day before yesterday, she got home around eleven at night or a bit later. Where was she coming from? From an evening at some friends' place, so and so and so and so, she gave me names; all of that could be verified. When had she seen Griselda for the last time? In the morning at breakfast; and then, when she came back at eleven, Griselda was dead and Memphis Charles had splattered blood all over herself trying to pick up the corpse with both hands, and then she saw the bloody knife and picked it up; she panicked; she got changed, went out, tossed the knife in the flower beds and her dirty clothes in the trash cans, and raced over to my place.

"Do you have any idea as to what Griselda had done during the day?"

She shook her head.

"No."

"You say that as if you two had had a spat."

"That's a fact."

"Because of that movie, *Daddy Longdick*?"

"Among other things."

"What other things?"

She shrugged and lit a cigarette. It wasn't one of the Marlboros from the car. She must have finished them. It was a Gauloise from a pack she'd just bought when she'd done her shopping (she opened the pack in front of me).

"Things in general," she groused. "Her lifestyle."

"She was slutty and she took acid. Is that it? Things like that?"

"Nothing specific like that. Each to her own, right? No, it was a question of the general spirit of things. She and I were not headed in the same direction. You know what I mean?"

I nodded. I started again from different angles. I tried to make the girl say if she knew people who wanted to hurt her friend. I asked her to try to remember if she'd seen something, anything, the least little noticeable detail, Monday night when she came home. And so on. She answered no to all my questions. Discouraging.

"You finished?"

I jumped. I hadn't noticed that I'd slipped into my own thoughts for several minutes.

"Yeah," I sighed.

"You're in the dark, right?"

Her voice was less hostile than ten minutes earlier. I nodded and grumbled sadly.

"We'd be better off going to the cops together, Tarpon," the kid said to me. "We've embarked on a tale of outlaws, me because I've read too many books and you because . . . I don't know. We'd be better off stopping right away."

"Give me until midnight," I said stubbornly.

"If you're afraid of sticking your neck out, I'll go alone and not mention you."

She'd already said that in the Toronado, in the middle of

the night, and it still didn't satisfy me. At this stage, there was no way I could come out smelling like roses. But I'd spent so much energy on this story that I just couldn't let things go. I stood up from the chair, shaking my head.

"I take back what I said. You're my client if that's what you want. Until midnight."

She took a checkbook out of one of the patch pockets on her suede thingy.

"How much do you get an hour?"

"No, it's free," I said.

I walked toward the door and said without turning around, "You'd be better off staying put here. Try to have a sandwich sent up. I'll call you."

I left the room. As I was about to close the door, I saw the kid standing up, the pajamas in hand. She made an odd little friendly grimace at me. I pulled the door shut.

I walked out of the hotel and back to the Aronde. I sat motionless at the wheel for a moment before starting the car. Then I headed toward the Seventeenth Arrondissement, where the guy named Eddy Alfonsino lived.

The small-time hood, a friend of Griselda about whom Gérard Sergent had spoken the previous day, lived in a charming freestone apartment building near the place Péreire. While a surprisingly slow elevator carried me up toward the top level, I was thinking that crime does pay, even if old Eddy could only afford a former maid's room converted into a "studio." I know it was a studio, and even an elegant studio, because the door was ajar and, because no one was answering the bell, I pushed the door open and saw the room, the mattress eviscerated, the end table on its side, the drawers upside down, the floor littered with papers and clothes, and Alfonsino dead on the carpet.

18

I couldn't go on like this. I used my ballpoint pen to lift the receiver. It fell next to the base, on top of the dressing table. I dialed a number with the pen and leaned my head over to talk into the thing without sticking my prints everywhere. I asked for Coquelet; I got Coccioli. The commissioner had gone out. I told the officer what I was calling about, where I was, and that I was waiting for him. He said he was on his way.

As I waited, I snooped around the mess, but most of what I could learn from the room was already visible. As for Eddy Alfonsino, who in his lifetime had been a big guy with a big nose who looked like an eagle turned vulture, with black hair and topaz eyes, he'd been stabbed with a knife in the heart. The blade had broken between his ribs. A square end stuck out from the tear in his purple silk pajamas and there wasn't a lot of blood. The corpse was on its back, head toward the door. The knife handle was nowhere to be seen; it must have left with the murderer some time ago; the blood was dry and brownish.

Under the bedside table were four small, rectangular marks. I looked closely and didn't need to touch them to know they were gummy. Adhesive tape or sticky paper. Exactly as if something had been stuck under the table with two pieces of adhesive paper that formed an x. So there were two possibilities: either that wasn't what the killer had been looking for when he came in here, or else the killer was a not the sharpest knife in the drawer because finally finding what you're looking for in such a pathetic hiding place is not the sign of a superior mind.

Opposite the front door was another, half-open door. I pushed on it with my knee. It opened onto a very small bathroom, with a hipbath. In the tub were an American Durst enlarger lying on its side and a variety of other photo supplies—paper, pieces of plastic basins. The whole thing seemed to have been diligently destroyed; the bottles of developer and other chemicals had been smashed on the bottom of the tub, forming a nasty, gooey mess.

There were no photos in sight, neither in the bathroom nor in the rest of the studio. The papers strewn on the floor seemed to be pages from a film script. I skimmed one or two. It was not a script meant for children.

The late Alfonsino's clothes were numerous, expensive, and stylish. I didn't examine them in detail. This time, I was sure I'd be hauled in, and I had to warn Memphis Charles. I tapped on the phone hook with my pen but then hesitated before dialing the number. As long as I could still use my two legs, I didn't want the kid to panic, and I wasn't entirely sure I was going to be put behind bars. In the end, I dialed Stanislavski's number. I could also have called Haymann, but his journalistic instincts bothered me. He had his own agenda, and I didn't want him in my backyard, so to speak.

At the sound of my voice, the brave little tailor went into a tizzy and started to tell me all about how he'd gone to my place, the comings and goings of the cops, and that he thought they had arrested "your journalist friend," and he wanted to know why I was calling, where I was, and what had happened to me. I had to interrupt him because I didn't have all the time in the world. I hoped I hadn't hurt his feelings.

"If I haven't called you before noon tomorrow," I explained, "call this number. It's a hotel. Ask for Mrs. Malone." That was the name the kid had used when she signed the register for us. "Tell the person I'm in prison and that I advise her to go to the police."

"You're in prison, Mr. Tarpon!"

"No, no," I said, "but it could happen. I'll tell you all about it in a day or two, or maybe even sooner. I don't have time now, sorry. So just tell her that I advise her to go to the police, but if she would rather go on vacation, I haven't said a word about her."

"Got it."

He repeated everything and promised to be punctual. I thanked him, apologized again, and hung up with my ballpoint. I'd just stepped away from the phone when Coccioli came in.

He had another plainclothes guy with him I'd never seen, and a disapproving sound came out of his mouth as he considered the corpse and the fucking mess in the room. He also had a uniformed cop with him, whom he told to wait on the landing. And of course there were two more downstairs.

The merry cop gazed at me and shook his head wearily. He didn't look furious; instead he seemed sad. Still, he had quite a few reasons to be pissed at me. His hair was shorter, not at all hepcat anymore; half of it must have burned off when those pro-Palestinian clowns attacked his car, and the barber could only make do with what was a fait accompli. In addition to yesterday's Band-Aid on his nose, Coccioli had a bandage on one cheek and another one on the back of his right hand. He noticed my stare.

"It's that ass of a butcher," he said. "He thought I was one of the guys who were attacking you. And I thought he was one."

"Sorry," I sighed.

"Not your fault."

His tone was not convincing. He looked at me wearily again.

"I'm going to have a lot of questions for you," he said. "That makes me feel better."

"I'm not sure I'll have all the answers."

"We'll find them together."

He shrugged. The rest of the team came in and cautiously spread out in the studio. The doc murmured that the dead guy was dead and that he'd probably been stabbed to death, all of which anyone could see. The other cop found the debris in the tub and called Coccioli to show it to him.

When he came back, to my astonishment, he led me downstairs. There was a bar down the street and we went in. I learned of late never to let an occasion to eat slip by, because you never know when the next one will come along. So I ordered a croque-monsieur and a beer. Coccioli ordered a coffee. For a minute or two he twirled his spoon in his cup pensively.

"Tell me what you've been up to since last night," he said at last. "Just the main points. If I want details, I'll ask for them."

"You won't believe me," I sighed between two bites of croque-monsieur.

He advised me not to be a naysayer and I explained that I'd been collared by a bunch of strangers, as he'd seen, and I hadn't had time to see their faces when they knocked me out; I came to when I heard gunshots.

"Gunshots?"

"I was tied to a bed in a bedroom in a secluded house," I said.

"How do you know it was secluded?"

"I found out afterwards. Let me go on."

He nodded. I continued.

"When I managed to get free, the shooting had stopped for a while. It was late at night, but I don't know exactly when. My watch had stopped."

"Well isn't that convenient!" Coccioli muttered.

I ignored him.

"I left the bedroom. I went through the house. I discovered two dead men."

Coccioli spilled a little coffee on the cuff of his shirtsleeve as he choked. Then he swore.

"Two dead men in addition to Alfonsino?"

I sighed affirmatively.

"There wasn't a soul in the place anymore," I explained. "Just the two corpses."

I said that I'd searched the bodies, that one was called Carbone and the other Ford and that they appeared to have killed each other. As I was saying this, Coccioli was rinsing his stained cuff with water from a carafe and sucking it to get the coffee out. It was disgusting. He was getting on my nerves.

"You didn't call the police," he noted.

"Let me explain how I see things. Did you look under the bedside table at Alfonsino's? Did you notice?"

"I did."

"The murderer filched something. All these people are running after something ever since Griselda Zapata was killed. Don't you agree?"

"I don't know."

"Something like a dangerous little black book," I insisted.

"Blackmail," said Coccioli. "Is that what you're thinking? Someone kills Louise Sergent to steal something, but she's not the one who has it, it's Alfonsino, because he was her pimp."

"I don't know if he was her pimp. I'm just hypothesizing."

"He was her pimp," Coccioli repeated emphatically.

"Okay. Let's say there was a dangerous little black book. We can imagine several people looking for it. We can imagine they nab me. We can imagine they fight each other. No?"

"You're not a dangerous little black book, Tarpon," Coccioli remarked.

I let out a weak sigh.

"But some people, including you cops, seem to think that I know where Memphis Charles is. And they might also think that Memphis Charles has the thingamajig that those people are looking for, a little black book or something else. Alfonsino might have been Louise Sergent's pimp, but Memphis Charles was her roommate."

Coccioli scratched his nose and blew on his cuff. He'd managed to make the stain on his cuff fade a little. He'd also managed to make it spread.

"To get back to your fairytale," he said, "according to you, two rival gangs were fighting over your precious self last night and nobody won and everybody disappeared, leaving you tied up in a bedroom and two dead men behind."

"I didn't say two rival gangs! The way I see it, there are only those two guys—the two dead guys—who stayed with me, and they must have had an argument because they each had their own idea about what to do with me and . . . and . . . and . . . that's it," I concluded pathetically.

"Don't you have a more plausible story to tell me?"

"I'm telling you what happened. It's not clear to me either!"

Coccioli sighed. He finished his coffee. He blew on the face of his watch and polished it with his right sleeve. He was exasperating.

"You didn't call the police," he remarked for the second time.

"I'd been seriously bopped on the head," I said, fingering my skull. "There was no phone in that house. I walked aimlessly. I tried to get cars to stop, but you know how people are. When a car finally stopped to pick me up, I didn't want to complicate things by asking to be driven to the nearest police station. I let myself be driven to Paris, and here I am."

"Here you are," Coccioli repeated, looking skeptically at his watch. "You think your story holds water?"

"No, but that's what happened."

Truth be told, I thought my story was outrageous. Now I was sure I was going to wind up behind bars. But Coccioli wasn't in a hurry. I suppose he was enjoying giving me the third degree.

"Why were you after Alfonsino?"

"You know perfectly well that Gérard Sergent hired me to find out about his sister. Obviously I need to ask people questions."

"You picked a good time. Luckily the concierge saw you go upstairs, and the blood is dry."

"I would have preferred to get there earlier and find the killer."

"You think the same person killed both Alfonsino and Louise Sergent?"

"Two murderers would be a lot," I noted.

"You're making no sense, Tarpon. You just told me that those two guys killed each other because of you last night."

He was right. I was not making sense. I tried to look offended. I told him the approximate location of the house where the bodies of Carbone and Ford were still most likely lying. He stood up.

"I'm going to make a phone call. Wait for me."

He left. I knew there was someone outside who would follow me if I took off. I didn't feel like getting nabbed for evading arrest. I was in it up to my ears as it was. I ordered another beer and another croque-monsieur.

When Coccioli came back from phoning, he looked disappointed to see me still there.

"I have to go back upstairs," he sighed. "We're going to check your story about a secluded house. You can stay and finish your lunch. Come up when you've finished."

He really wanted me to beat it.

"I'll come with you now," I said, quickly stuffing the second half of my snack into my mouth.

He glared at me. I swept everything down my gullet with a big gulp of beer. I paid for my lunch and the cop's coffee at the counter, and we climbed back up to Alfonsino's.

The cops had worked hard while we were gone, without much result. They'd found the late Eddy's lovely collection of cameras of all shapes and sizes, but not a single print. That made sense.

We were leaving the building just when a patrol wagon drove up to take the body away. Coccioli and the other cop whose name I didn't know shoved me into a Simca 1000 and took me back to the station with them.

It was in his office—or, more precisely, Coquelet's office—that Coccioli got the answer to the phone call he'd made at the bar. I was sitting down and I saw him snicker into the receiver. He said thanks and hung up. He turned toward me.

"So, Tarpon, are you nuts or what?"

I didn't understand the question. I said so.

"Don't play innocent," Coccioli ordered. "We found your secluded house. There's no one in it, dead or alive. It's for sale, if you're interested."

I shook my head, horrified.

"They must have . . . someone must have cleaned up," I stuttered.

Coccioli stood up, pounding the desktop with his palm. It looked like he was about to scold me, then an unreadable expression crossed his face. He scratched his nose. His bandage seemed to be itching him.

"Who would make up such a story?" he asked softly, his eyes unfocused.

I spread my hands and opened my lips to show my total agreement. Coccioli sat back down, still with a dreamy air.

"Listen, Tarpon. I'm happy to do whatever Coquelet tells me to. Get it?"

"Yes."

"That doesn't mean I wouldn't like to help you out."

"I know," I said.

"If only you could tell me where Memphis Charles is," he sighed.

"If only I could!" I agreed.

He looked at me as if he were heartbroken.

"Where will you go if I release you now?" he asked.

"To question other people who knew Griselda Zapata. Other people besides Alfonsino."

He asked me for names. I gave them to him. He knew

them already. His mood grew darker. He told me that, in a nutshell, he wasn't going to let me go right away because he wanted to review the matter again with me, as brothers, so as to be sure not to have forgotten anything. We reviewed the matter, again. Several times. At about five in the afternoon, I was nodding off. Coquelet arrived and took over. Coccioli left to throw back a few.

"Coccioli is a terrible muddler," Coquelet explained to me with a warm, kind voice. "He's too eager to do things properly. It'll be his downfall. He's too hungry. As for me, I'm prepared to let you go home while we wait for you to appear before the examining magistrate."

"Okay," I said.

"I'd just like for you to tell me where Memphis Charles is."

"I'd like to be able to," I said.

"You can't?"

"I can't."

"Professional secret?"

"Total ignorance."

He scratched his nose too, and he didn't even have a bandage on it.

"Fine," he said. "Let's start at the beginning."

19

AT SIX thirty that evening, they suddenly had a change of heart. In the meantime, cops from the Val d'Oise had gone through the abandoned house with a fine-toothed comb. No corpses, no traces of bullets (even the door had been changed), but I'd left two very legible fingerprints, and the Memphis kid had left a ton. I only learned about all that later. All I knew at the time was that good old Coquelet told me I was free to leave. I thought he'd taken the time to weave a spectacular web of guys to tail me. Which was true.

I started walking toward Chatelet. I was exhausted and sweaty. It was chilly and damp, and I was shaking like a leaf. I was totally dumbfounded. The deeper I got into this whole mess, the farther I was from understanding any of it.

I went down into the Métro. Given that my brain had turned to mush, the best thing I could do for the moment was to follow the plan I'd devised. At least in the Métro I warmed up instantly.

Thunder Films, the company owned by the producers Lyssenko and Vacher, sat on a sloped street west of Saint-Lazare station and as I walked I tried to figure out who was tailing me. Nothing doing. No doubt they were working in shifts. For the time being, I didn't give a damn. I was saving a little unexpected detour for later.

I was surprised to find the Thunder Films offices still open because it was after seven, but they were. An automatic door stood at the rear of a paved courtyard and I entered a carpeted lobby no bigger than my kitchen, with a small desk and some shelving. On the shelves were round cans made of tin or aluminum; the walls were covered in movie posters on which, among other niceties, girls in corsets swooned in the arms of strong brutes. Behind the tiny desk, at a typewriter, sat a very unsexy secretary, gray-haired, matchstick thin, but with a twinkle in her eye. I told her I wanted to see Mr. Vacher or Mr. Lyssenko.

"Do you have an appointment?"

"No."

"They're not here."

"I need to see them tonight," I said.

"If it's for the extras," the lady stated, "we're done hiring."

I said it wasn't for the extras, that I was representing Griselda Zapata's brother.

"Poor little thing. It's just horrible."

I nodded.

"Still, you can't see anyone this evening," she continued, losing her look of condolence. "Give me your name. You'll need to call tomorrow afternoon to get an appointment with Mr. Lyssenko."

"What about Vacher?" I asked. "Isn't he in?"

"He's in Germany, sir."

I could tell I was beginning to annoy the lady.

"And Lyssenko? Is he in Germany too?"

"No, but he's shooting."

"Shooting?"

"A movie, sir."

"Where?"

"You can't disturb him when he's shooting."

"Do you want a public scandal?" I asked.

Her eyes grew wide. She had no idea what I was talking about. Neither did I, but I looked like I did.

"I'm sure Lyssenko would prefer to see me discreetly this evening rather than at dawn tomorrow in the presence of the police," I said in a cruel and menacing tone.

She concentrated.

"Fine," she said with a flat voice. "Since it's so urgent..."

She gave me an address in Garches.

"They'll be there until midnight."

"Thanks," I said.

I hadn't sat down. I turned around, went out the door, and stood very still. I waited about thirty seconds then re-opened the door. The lady was on the phone and cut short her conversation, open-mouthed.

"Tell him it's not worth trying to get away," I said as I closed the door.

I went back toward Saint-Lazare on foot. It wasn't very nice of me to have fun terrifying people, but I needed to de-stress after my time with the cops.

At Saint-Lazare I bought a round-trip ticket and had a little less than fifty francs left in my pocket. I still had Gérard Sergent's check on me. I thought I'd better cash it before the big boy decided to fire me for incompetence.

On the train, I tried to locate the guy or guys who were tailing me. Coquelet could not possibly have extended his web to the suburbs. So there was a good chance that several of his guys got on the train at the same time as I did. I entertained myself by walking through the crowded train, but there were lots of people doing that, people who had gotten on at the back of the train just before it pulled away and who were cutting their way through the crowd toward the front, because that's where the exit of the station where they were getting off was located. Hopeless situation.

I got off at Garches with quite a few others. I stayed on the platform until the train took off again, which necessarily divided my guardian angels into three groups. Those who stayed on the train in case I'd gotten back on had left with it and were out of my hair. I had a good chance of picking out the ones who were waiting in the waiting room or the lavatory for me to keep moving. And in fact, when I reached the exit of the waiting room, I saw a young guy with a moustache hurrying to follow me. He passed me and disappeared outside the station. Then there was the third faction, the guy or guys who had managed to get out as soon as the train pulled in to wait for me outside.

I looked at a map in front of the station to orient myself as best I could. Night had gently fallen during the trip from Saint-Lazare to Garches. There was still a lot of car and foot traffic. I didn't see the guy with the moustache anymore.

I had to walk quite a ways before I reached the address the secretary at Thunder Films had given me. I realized I was getting really exhausted when I tripped on a broken sidewalk and found myself facedown on the ground. I stood up, brushed myself off, and walked on. There was nothing else to do. My knee was killing me.

The streets became fancier and fancier and more residential. The houses and small apartment buildings were set back from the sidewalk, lost behind curtains of greenery. I walked as quickly as I could to tire out the guys tailing me. The pedestrian traffic was thinning out and there were very few cars. I found my mustachioed guy; I also realized I was dealing with another female cop when twice in fifteen minutes, at a distance of two kilometers, I passed the same housewife with the same shopping bag.

Just before 9:00 p.m. I reached the place—a white house surrounded by huge grounds. It occupied the entire space bordered by three streets that intersected obliquely. From outside the property, among the trees and bushes, you could barely make out the house. But in front of the house you could see there was a lot of blinding light. Spotlights. Silhouettes, totally pale in the light, were moving about.

I located the front door. I was expecting to find several vicious doorkeepers, but no, I walked right in and quickly joined a group of people busying themselves near the spotlights. Blinded, I bumped into something and fell down on all fours for the second time in less than an hour. Gravel pierced my palms. I was furious.

"Some asshole took a nosedive on the traveling platform," a disgusted voice announced.

"Sorry," I said as I got up, walking away fast from a guy who wanted to help me up. (Good Lord, I wasn't an old man. Not yet anyway).

I explained I'd come to see Lyssenko. Just then someone yelled from the house to ask if everyone was ready. Everyone answered yeah, including the fellow I'd been talking to, who took me by the arm and pushed me between two bushes.

"Stay there. Don't move. Wait."

He left me and raced off to accomplish some mysterious task. A big guy wearing a teal suit and a blue-and-white-striped tie strolled out of the French doors of the house, crossed the balcony, and jumped onto the gravel a dozen meters away, in the shadows, where he seemed to be conferring with the others. I couldn't see much and understood even less. There were all sorts of fantastic cries like "Action" and "Rolling" and more. Then a girl came out of the house and walked onto the balcony. She was wearing a transparent negligee with red panties underneath. She had voluptuous charms and the face of a sheep. The big guy in blue kept shouting at her from the shadows.

"Walk forward! Slower! Look around you! You're starting to get worried! You're about to shiver! Place your hand on your throat as you stare into the night! Stare more slowly! That's it! Now call him..."

"Fabrice?" she called in an off-key singsongy voice.

No one answered.

"Bang!" shouted the man in blue after a moment of silence.

The girl let out a cry and placed her hands on her generous bosom. I got an odd shock watching the hemoglobin spurt between her fingers. She fell forward, very awkwardly, onto a mattress.

"Cut!" the man in blue ordered and several voices agreed that it was well done, which was somewhat of an exaggeration, and someone else announced that he had to reload. The lights were dimmed and everyone started talking and smoking. The dead girl stood up and ran back into the house. Before she disappeared, she sneezed loudly.

"Shit," she said. "I've got such a fucking cold."

I thought it was a good time to go see the big guy in blue, which I did, but not without getting my feet caught in all sorts of electrical wires.

"Mr. Lyssenko?" I asked.

"Yeah? Whaddya want?"

He was leafing through a sheaf of mimeographed pages. The script, I suppose.

"Get number thirty-eight ready," he ordered his entourage before I had time to answer.

The entourage scattered.

"Can I have a moment of your time?" I asked. "I represent Griselda Zapata's brother."

"The poor kid," Lyssenko said without missing a beat. "What a horrible way to go. We were very fond of her. Follow me."

He hopped on the balcony in a single bound. It was a good fifty centimeters above the yard and I needed to use one of my hands to climb up. Lyssenko was already striding into the house. I rushed to follow him.

We passed through a room full of wires where the victim from the earlier scene, bundled in a tweed coat, was drinking mulled wine with a Bantu who was two meters tall.

"We're shooting number thirty-eight in fifteen minutes," Lyssenko said to them, still walking.

We exited the room through the back. I followed the man up a narrow staircase. At the top was a corridor. He opened a door and stepped aside to let me pass. I entered a kind of office where sheets of paper were strewn about on the carpet. I heard Lyssenko shut the door behind me and I turned around just in time to catch his fat fist on my jaw.

The punch sent me flying against the wall and I banged my head.

"So, you little bastard," said Lyssenko, walking toward me. "You want to blackmail me?"

He was around forty years old and in top physical shape. At a guess, I'd say a hundred kilos of muscle and bone in a package a meter eighty tall. His complexion was pink and healthy, his hair short, his jaw square, and his hands like anvils. If I hadn't caught the first punch, I think he would've broken my face. I took out my ballpoint pen.

"Back off or I'll shove it in your eye," I said.

He was about to crush me against the wall, but he hesitated. I'd made my voice hysterical and quavering.

"What's this nonsense about blackmail?" I asked in a more sober tone.

He waddled from one foot to the other, striking one palm with his other fist. The vein in his temple throbbed. He seemed not to want to abandon the idea of beating me to a pulp. With my left hand, I took out my wallet and threw it at him.

"Take a look," I said. "Then I'll put away my pen, you'll put away your big paws, and perhaps we can have a calm conversation."

He looked. He calmed down. He sat behind the desk and placed my wallet on one of the desk corners. He opened a drawer and took out two glasses, a carafe, and a box of cigars. He took a quick drink, no doubt to calm his nerves, then he poured some liquor in the other glass and refilled his.

"Let's start at the beginning," he said. "And, um, I apologize. When I'm shooting, I'm very nervous. I'm an artist, you know…"

I nodded. He looked about as much like an artist as a regiment of foreign legion parachutists. I unstuck myself from the wall and cast a nervous glance at it, in case my outline had made a hole in it, like you see in cartoons. My jaw was sending waves of pain through my head and shoulders.

"What's this nonsense about blackmail?" I repeated, pulling a chair toward me with my foot.

I sat down. He held out a glass to me across the desk. I sniffed. It was Armagnac. It wouldn't cure my headache.

"Let's not mention it again," he said. "What brings you here? You're representing Griselda Zapata's brother, you said?"

I said I was, that I was trying to investigate her murder,

and that I wanted to know what he thought about it. He raised his arms to the sky.

"What I think, Mr. . . . Tarpon? I don't think anything! I'm an honest businessman taking care of business, that's all."

He looked at his watch.

"I'd like to help you," he stated. "Unfortunately . . ."

"Yeah, sure," I said. "You don't give a fuck."

He laughed. And looked at me through his laughter.

"Private detective, huh? I suppose that it's not a very romantic job?"

"You're so right."

"I've got something for you, by George! I've got something!"

He laughed again, or else he was laughing about something ahead of time. It must have been a good joke. He leaned over to pick up a briefcase under the desk. He placed it in front of him, opened it, and took out an envelope from which he pulled a photograph and a letter. He handed them to me.

The photograph, sixteen by twenty-three centimeters, was folded in half to fit in the envelope. Despite the line of the fold, it was easy to recognize the producer-director and the bleached blond. Griselda Zapata, alive and well, and Lyssenko, just as alive and well, were wearing almost nothing and giving themselves over to the carnal act in an extremely bizarre way, with the help of a four-poster bed and a trapeze.

"Look at the letter," Lyssenko told me.

I quickly put down the photo and examined the letter, which had been written with a typewriter, its elite typeface dirty and worn-out, on a sheet of Basseau Extra Strong (sixty-four grams per square meter) paper, as far as I could tell at first glance. The text wasn't dated and there was no letterhead or signature.

Disgusting fat pig (it said) the photo I've attached here will tell you that I know your rotten vices Do you want these vices to show up on the front page of the papers Or do you want your wife to get a copy in the mail or under your door I KNOW EVERYTHING ABOUT YOU YOU DIRTY ROT-TEN BASTARD You cannot buy innocence because it only belongs to the innocent You can only atone First you have to stop your filth Then you have to take two million old francs from your bank account leave your office tomorrow Thursday at four o'clock with the money Drive to Montpar-nasse station and put the two million in the locker the key to which is attached here AT EXACTLY FIVE O'CLOCK Your every move is being watched Don't try to escape your FATE but ATONE ATONE YOU SCUM and I will forgive you and destroy the negative I SPIT ON YOU

"This was attached," Lyssenko said when I raised my eyes from the letter, and he opened his palm and showed me a flat key. "Now you understand," he added. "That letter got on my nerves. My secretary called me a little while ago to tell me that some character was coming to see me, threaten-ing to kick up a public stink. I made a mistake."

"You shouldn't have showed me that," I said. "You're too trusting."

He broke out laughing

"Why would I give a shit? So I fuck floozies. What about it? The guy trying to blackmail me with this is a repressed asshole. End of story."

"He could cause you problems on the home front," I sug-gested.

He broke out laughing again.

"That pervert has no idea what he's talking about. I've been divorced for six years and it's not the little hussies I'm a sugar daddy to who are going to be jealous. 'I know every-thing about you,' he said. Don't make me laugh."

He laughed. I let him.

"When did you get this?" I asked when he'd finished laughing.

"A little while ago. At the office. By pneumatic tube."

He held out the envelope to me. The pneumatic came from the Seventeenth Arrondissement in Paris. Not too far from Alfonsino's. It had been sent at two in the afternoon when Alfonsino was already cold and in the hands of the cops. It was interesting.

"I have to go back down," said Lyssenko as he finished his Armagnac. "I hope you've gotten some food for thought tonight. I understand you'd like to ask me a bunch of ques-tions about our Griselda, but I've got work to do. If you'd like to call me in the office tomorrow in the late morning, we can make an appointment."

"Just a second," I said. "Do you know a certain Eddy Alfonsino?"

"Yes."

"Could he have taken the picture?"

Lyssenko stood up. He knit his brown eyebrows and I could tell he was digging through his memory, or else he was doing a good imitation.

"Eddy Alfonsino would never write a letter like that. He's an idiot, but he's not stupid."

"That's not what I'm asking."

He thought hard again.

"Yeah," he sighed. "Eddy could have taken the picture. Little bastard."

"How long ago?"

"Eight months ago. When we were filming *Forbidden Caresses*. But believe me, he's not the one who sent the letter."

"I know," I said.

He raised an eyebrow but didn't ask for details. I put my wallet back in my pocket, and he put away the letter and the dirty picture, and we went down to the ground floor together. I couldn't hang around. I didn't represent the law, as they say. I said I'd call him in the late morning. I asked him if he could find out, discreetly, between now and then if other people in his circle had received the same kind of package. He absentmindedly promised to do so. I could tell that he wouldn't. We said our goodbyes. It was ten at night and I didn't want to make the crying man wait too long.

20

THE MUSTACHIOED guy who was tailing me was loitering in the shadows behind the parked cars. I didn't want to bring him, or his pals, to the crying man. The Ottoman detritus might've taken offense at their presence, or else Coquelet's boys might've suddenly decided to pounce on the detritus to ask him a few questions, none of which appealed to my gut intuition.

Nonetheless, I strolled back calmly to the train station in Garches. My stalkers had all the time in the world to gather round me and support each other. When I climbed aboard the train to Saint-Lazare I saw the mustachioed guy get on as well, along with the fishy housewife still carrying her shopping bag and two or three other characters far from kosher.

They were probably quite surprised when, in the dark station at Bécon-les-Bruyères, just as the doors were closing and the train was pulling out, I suddenly dived into the opening in the double doors, jumped down onto the platform, and raced toward the exit. The ticket taker who should have been at the spot where I ran like the wind wasn't even there anymore. I cast a quick glance over my shoulder and saw the unshakable mustachioed guy speeding to catch up to me. No one else. I leapt out onto the public thoroughfare. My knee was killing me, my head ached, and my calves were wobbly. I ran. Several kilometers. My heart had doubled in size by the time I'd crossed the Pont de Levallois, still running. At the end of the bridge, as you know, there's a subway stop by the same name. I had tickets in my pocket. I barged onto the platform. Finally I had the luck I'd been waiting for: a train ready to leave. I catapulted inside. I was wheezing. The train began to leave the station. I rested my warm forehead against a cool window and saw my mustachioed guy, blue with rage and red with exhaustion, abandoning the idea of jumping the turnstile. The train took off down the dark tunnels.

At the Pereire stop, I sprinted out of the subway and into the street. Haymann's Aronde was waiting patiently where I'd left it when I'd gone up to Alfonsino's. I hopped in without bothering to remove the parking ticket on the windshield. Like a good little girl, the car started on the fourth try. I headed to Champ-de-Mars.

I managed to park near a crosswalk less than a hundred meters from the Hilton. This rash of good luck was starting to worry me.

As I entered the hotel, a young guy I was sure I'd seen before on movie posters was coming out. A retinue of guys his age in checkered suits, a slew of bellhops, and a few photographers snapping away followed close behind him. The young guy and his retinue piled into two supple, shiny Silver Ghosts. So, I thought, nothing could happen to me in such a classy joint. I went over to reception.

They considered me suspiciously because I looked a bit frayed around the edges. But there was a message for me, Tarpon. A certain Louis Caruso was waiting for me at the bar of the restaurant on the roof.

I took the elevator. It was exactly 11:00 p.m. when I walked into the restaurant. A huge crowd was eating at this ungodly hour, and Stéphane Grappelli was playing "Sweet Georgia Brown." Caruso stood up immediately, even before the staff offered to guide me to a table (or kick me out because my shirt collar looked dodgy). Caruso's collar didn't look dodgy in the least. He was wearing a salmon-colored tux, like a musician in a dance band. He glared at me.

"We're going down," he said.

His accent was much more accentuated than the defunct Pappy Ruger's. I hesitated.

"We go only to apartment here," he added. "Better for you friendly conversation, no?"

I conceded. Once again I couldn't imagine getting bumped off in such a high-class joint. We took the elevator down together. Three or four stories later, we got out, went along a corridor without a single window, which made me feel slightly claustrophobic. Or afraid. Caruso rang the bell at one of the doors. The guy who I'd seen at the wheel of the Mercedes opened it. We went into a vestibule.

"May I?" asked Caruso as he started to pat me down.

I sighed, took off my watch, took out my ballpoint, my keys, and Haymann's ignition key and gave them to him.

"Would you like my belt and shoelaces too?" I asked.

"No thank you," said the Mercedes driver. "Come."

We passed through the vestibule into an apartment. It was a nice place with a balcony from which you could see the illuminated Eiffel Tower. The crying man was sitting in a leather armchair in front of a coffee table where a bottle of cognac, glasses, a soda siphon, and a bucket of ice were waiting. He wasn't crying. His big eyes were still bloodshot, but all the rest of him seemed more normal than before. Cleaner too. He was clean-shaven and I suspected he'd put on some sort of powder, but there was nothing effeminate about him. He was wearing a flame-colored silk smoking jacket, black slacks, and a freshly ironed collarless white shirt. He was smoking a Manila cigar. He looked at me.

"Hello, Monsieur Tarpon," he said in a clear and careful voice, without a noticeable accent.

I nodded a greeting and crossed the living room, which was vast.

"I see you got my message," he remarked, pointing to the other armchair.

I sat down, trying to look confident. The crying man was gazing at me thoughtfully. And continued gazing at me in silence. Were we about to go another round?

"Are we about to go another round?" I asked.

"Another round? I don't understand," the man said. "Monsieur Tarpon, please forgive me if my understanding of French is restricted to everyday expressions, some basic slang, and the language of business. Explain now. Another round?"

"You're not going to start staring at me without a word again, are you?"

"No."

"So who are you?" I asked.

"My name is Marius Gorizia. I'm an American citizen. I'm a powerful businessman, if you see what I mean."

"I do."

"Spare me the pathetic chitchat," he declared in an even tone. "My nerves are on edge. I'm looking for someone so I can destroy him. I'm prepared to destroy several people if necessary. You don't amuse me. Your existence is merely a burden to me. Do you understand?"

"I understand your words."

"If you find my words ridiculous," he stated, "it's because you don't know how powerful I am."

"That's possible," I said. "Did you dispose of the corpses of your two henchmen? Is that what sets your nerves on edge?"

"I am not amused!"

He was shouting.

"Neither am I!" I shouted back.

He slapped the side of his armchair several times, hard. He was trembling. With rage, it would seem. He looked like a malicious, angry child. He was scaring me a little. Then suddenly he calmed down.

"Yes, as a matter of fact," he sighed. "Ford and Carbone have been taken away and destroyed. They are no longer of interest to us. You are."

"You interest me too," I answered politely.

"I want Memphis Charles," Marius Gorizia said.

I rubbed my knee. It was still hurting.

"What for?"

He didn't answer.

"To destroy her?" I suggested.

"You obviously know where she is," he stated as a response. "I'll pay you for the information."

"A million new francs," I threw out.

He considered it. My word, he seriously considered it! Then he shook his head.

"No. You're joking. That's too much. Fifty thousand, that's what I'm offering. Final offer. I can obtain the information using less gentle means, but I prefer the simplicity of money. It can buy everything."

"May I?" I said and poured myself a cognac without waiting for the answer. "Tell me why you want Memphis Charles."

"I want to look at her."

"The way you looked at me?"

"Exactly."

He wasn't joking. It was crazy.

"And that's all?" I asked.

"The rest will depend on what I see when I look at her."

He raised his glass in my direction.

"Cheers," he added warmly and downed his cognac in one gulp.

I took a sip of mine. With fifty thousand francs, how long can a person live in peace? Marius Gorizia, I thought, could spend them in a week. It would take some people a year. As for me, with my lifestyle, even supposing I bought a car, I'd still have enough left to live off of for two years. And could even get in a month's vacation in a good hotel on the Mediterranean. I took another sip of cognac. How long can a person live on fifty thousand with the memory of someone you sold down the river?

"What's your goal?" I asked.

"I just told you."

"No. Your final goal."

His face tensed. He poured himself another cognac and was about to swallow that one too, but then he put his glass back down.

"I want to kill the little girl's murderer," he said at last in a monotone.

"Little girl" isn't exactly the term I would have used.

"Griselda Zapata?" I asked for confirmation.

He confirmed. I finished my cognac.

"Why?" I asked.

He shook his head.

"You're not telling me the truth. You're not telling the truth about anything," I said angrily, and my anger surprised me. I didn't know why I felt suddenly so pissed off, and I was hot.

He shot me a withering glance and got out of his armchair. He walked toward me. I wanted to stand. He placed his palm on my face and his fingers closed around my jaw. He pushed me sideways. I made a move to defend myself, and the glass of cognac slipped from my hand and flew through the air. It shattered on the coffee table. Gorizia pushed me over the side of the armrest and I landed on my back on the carpet. I wanted to get up but I couldn't. It was the cognac. Or something in it. In my glass. I looked at the shards on the table, far above me.

"Bastard," I managed to sputter.

The detritus laughed softly, gently. He was on all fours on the floor, leaning over me. I could smell his aftershave.

"Now you're relaxed," he purred. "I'm your friend. Don't struggle against the warmth of the limbo you're in."

He bent my knees and my arms against my torso and slowly rolled me onto my side. He got up for a second, and then I was wrapped in a soft, silky cloth, maybe a bathrobe.

"You're limply, pleasantly, becoming an embryo again," Gorizia murmured in my ear. "You're back in your mother's womb. It's warm. It's liquid. You don't exist yet. You have no responsibilities. I'm your friend. You can ask me anything. You can tell me everything. I'm your darling mommy."

I could still understand that what he was telling me wasn't true; but the feeble notion I had about that was dwindling. I knew I had to hold on, but I couldn't manage to hold on to anything. I was fine. Fine. Warm. Innocent. I was innocent.

Voilà! That was it!

That's what I could hold on to, for Pete's sake!

Innocent! Hah! Sweat and noise. Shouting. Banners. It's better to be rich and healthy than poor and from the Breton countryside. Shouting. Various projectiles. Foran got a rotten vegetable tossed at him. His face was dripping with it. He swears but I don't hear him because of the shouts coming from the crowd. His face looks awful, but not because of the vegetable; it's his expression. Hatred. Shouts. Hatred. Hatred. I. Hatred. There's a grenade in my VB rifle. Shouts. Cobblestone. I'm hit. Blood. Fire! Blood. Blood. Death. Retreat inside the prefecture. Prefecture, fucking shit!

I retreat inside the prefecture where everything is dark and silent for a long long very long time...

"...we'll never get anything out of him. He's holding on to something," said Gorizia.

I understood what he was saying. Yet he was speaking American. I'd studied a bit of English in night school. Obviously I'd forgotten everything, but I suppose if someone goes rummaging through your brain, a bunch of things rise to the surface, like in a pond. Gorizia was speaking to someone. I could only grasp bits and pieces for the moment. I was rising toward reality. The present. The surface of the pond. My brief mastery of modern languages was gone. I had a miserable hangover. Dry mouth. I was on the floor, sweating, wrapped in a silk bathrobe. Perspiration dripped in my eyes and mouth. I closed my mouth. Another voice—not Gorizia's—spoke. My eyes were closed but I felt someone leaning over me, placing a stethoscope on my heart. My eyelids fluttered open. The guy stood up. He was young, wearing a tweed suit and glasses with black rectangular frames, and carrying a leather satchel. He moved away from me. Standing, he looked down at me, then turned to converse with Gorizia who seemed exhausted and despondent. After a while, the young guy left. Gorizia came back to lean over me and handed me a glass of cognac.

"This one isn't drugged," he stated, and I believed him because his voice was that of a defeated man.

I drank it. It burned my mouth and warmed my insides.

I closed my eyes an instant. I heard Gorizia explaining to me that I'd scared him because I'd had convulsions in my sleep. Apparently everyone else relaxed when old Marius offered his evening potion. I, on the other hand, had slept too deeply. That's why he wound up calling his private doctor. How kind of him.

"So you definitely don't want to tell me where Memphis Charles is?"

"No," I managed to utter.

"Listen, Tarpon," said Marius. "I simply want justice to be done. I just want to find the little girl's murderer. The first two people I thought of were you and that old reporter, Haymann, right? Because you were there. But it can't be Haymann because he was at a police station when the murder occurred. And you, I looked at you and I know that you're not capable of that kind of murder."

"I killed a man once," I muttered. "And I killed Patrick Ford."

"I know that," Marius murmured. "But the circumstances were different. I got information about you and I know it was different. I looked at you for a long time and I know you didn't kill the little girl."

"You do, huh?" I snarled. "It's that simple? You look and you know what a man has in his heart?"

"I didn't say exactly that."

True, he hadn't said exactly that. I sighed. I managed to sit up. I was aching all over. I drank some more cognac.

"Do you want some coffee?" Marius asked.

I nodded. He picked up the phone and ordered coffee

from downstairs. I looked at him as he spoke. His beard had started to come in.

"Good Lord!" I cried. "What time is it?"

Then I realized there was daylight behind the blinds, even though the lamps inside were lit. I wanted to get up and I fell back down on the carpet.

"Take it easy," said Marius as he hung up the phone. "Your heart needs to rest. Because of the drug. Please forgive me."

"What time is it, for God's sake!" I said again. "Where's my watch, you swine?"

"It's noon."

I was shocked.

"Yes," said Marius. "It lasted a really long time. That's why, I swear, I was worried and I called my doctor."

Twelve hours out cold! With convulsions! No wonder I was stiff and achy all over! And I'd thought it had lasted fifteen minutes...

"I have to make a call," I stammered.

I had to call Memphis Charles. But I couldn't. Not from here. I had to call Stanislavski. Tell him not to make the call to the kid that I'd asked him to. I hoped it wasn't too late.

"I'll make the call for you," said Marius obligingly.

I looked at him. I felt my facial muscles relax.

"Don't bother," I said.

I'd managed to get up on my knees, and Marius was observing my efforts with an air of reproach when the coffee arrived. Caruso came in from the vestibule where he'd grabbed the coffee and placed it on the coffee table. It was delicious. Caruso left. I poured myself three cups in a row. I was recharged. I gripped an armchair and pulled myself up, shaking my head to get rid of the cobwebs left in my brain.

"I'm leaving," I said.

"You haven't told me where to find Memphis Charles."

"And I won't tell you."

"I swear I only want to look at her, Tarpon. I'll be able to tell if she could be the killer."

"Have you seen a lot of killers in your life?" I asked sarcastically.

My sarcasm was lost on him. Marius nodded very seriously.

"Yes, of course," he said.

"What kind of businessman are you exactly?" I asked. "Mafia kind?"

"Mafia, organized crime, all that is bullshit," Marius answered. "But, yes, I've seen a lot of killers. I'd be able to recognize one."

"Was Griselda Zapata blackmailing you?" I asked on impulse.

He looked at me, horrified.

"You're mad!" he shouted. "My little girl!"

21

HE STARTED to cry.

That's when I realized he didn't have any allergies, as I'd thought the day before yesterday. He was crying like the last time I'd seen him in the gadget-filled Mercedes. Water poured out of his eyes, ran down his face, dripped from his chin onto the carpet. What had he said a moment, or hours, ago? Nerves on edge. Indeed.

He sat down in his armchair and blew his nose in a silk handkerchief.

"…C-c-can't…C-c-can't talk anymore," he said in a fairly calm voice.

I watched him cry. I felt like a shit. Marius Gorizia was most definitely a royal scumbag. But I felt sorry for him. My peasant roots, I suppose. I could understand a sense of family and mourning. I got hold of myself.

"Louise Sergent," I said. "Your daughter."

He nodded, sending tears flying in all directions. He stood abruptly. He walked over to a set of drawers. He opened a drawer violently. He took out a black cardboard box decorated with white emblems that looked more or less Masonic. He took from the box a multicolored wooden cube. He pressed his thumb on the top of the cube and it fell apart. Different colored rods with indentations fell onto the carpet. Marius picked up the rods, sat back down across from me in his armchair, and began to reassemble the cube by gathering the rods. On the side of the black box it said "Maddening Brainteaser." I suppose it calmed Marius down.

"I served as a captain in the US Army," he said. "Lord knows, that Madam Sergent was a fucking whore!"

He'd almost shouted. I suppose that that too could be a way to calm oneself down. All while speaking, he continued to reassemble the oddly shaped little sticks or logs, fitting them together almost without looking.

"The father, that is, Mr. Sergent, wound up hanging himself, see?" he said casually. "His daughter wasn't really his. His son either. People were laughing at him. Poor stupid little French peasant."

"Are you Gérard's father too?" I asked.

"Gérard?" He seemed blindsided. "Oh, the little brother. No, no. I'd already been gone for some time. Later I got news. I kept informed. I became more and more important in America, see? I didn't have time to take care of the little girl. I should be forgiven for that."

I nodded. It seemed like the thing to do. He went on.

"This was the first year I could come. Maybe I shouldn't have. It's risky for my business in the States if I'm gone. But I came because I knew my little girl was in a fix. Is that the right word?"

"Yes," I said. "She had problems."

"Pink movies."

"Blue," I corrected him.

"Blue movies. And her friends. Pigs, right? Eddy Alfonsino and people like that. So I came. She didn't know I was her dad. I started having her watched before going to see her. And the exact night we started watching over her, she was killed."

He'd finished his brainteaser. He tossed the cube in a corner of the room. The cube fell apart in some twenty little pieces. Marius opened his arms.

"Killed," he repeated.

The waterworks started again. His lips were moving, but no sound was coming out. I'd stopped feeling sorry for him. I poured another cognac in my coffee cup and drank it down.

"And you want to find the killer," I said. "To destroy him."

He nodded, wiping his face with his handkerchief.

"And you think it might be Memphis Charles," I added.

"Don't you, Tarpon?"

"No."

"Can you prove it?"

I shrugged.

"It's because of the faked rape," he explained. "Like a woman who wanted it to look like it was the work of a man. You understand? You know?"

"I know," I said. "But you? How do you know?"

"Ah, Tarpon," he said, sighing. "I told you, I'm powerful. When I want information, I get it."

He nodded energetically, but seemed completely shattered. When all is said and done, this was turning out to be an odd interrogation—it was taking place backwards. I mean, I was going to be the one who learned something, and old Marius was no further along than when we started. I stood up. I could now move rather easily.

"I really have to go," I said.

"No," he murmured. "I want Memphis Charles right now. The less you want to turn her over to me, the more I think I need her. Get it?"

I got it.

"I get it," I said. "Still, the answer is no. I'm leaving."

"Luigi!" old Marius hollered.

The door to the vestibule opened immediately and the guy named Louis Caruso came in. Old Marius said something to him in American. Caruso looked at me and there was a glimmer of satisfaction in his eyes. He walked up to me.

"We're not gonna fight here," I said. "Not in the Hilton. You'll get arrested, my friend."

Caruso was moving forward and I was backing up toward the window. In one quick, smooth motion he pulled a new piece from his collection of metal tools out of his side pocket. A Colt New Police Python. It makes holes as big as its name. Not even a silencer, which wouldn't have served much purpose anyway on a revolver. And I was scared, very scared. And then the bell rang, I mean the telephone.

Caruso stood still. He was blinking spasmodically, like an owl in the sun. Except I don't know if owls have eyelids to blink with.

Marius picked up the phone. He listened. He wrinkled his brow and glanced at me, preoccupied.

"Okay. Thanks."

He hung up.

"It's okay, Luigi," Marius said (or something like that), and Caruso nodded somewhat disappointedly and went out of the room, stuffing his Colt in his pants pocket.

Marius looked at me dispassionately.

"I know where Memphis Charles is," he said, in French again.

I didn't answer. I didn't believe him. I thought it was another trick to make me talk.

"She's been arrested," said Marius. "I was just speaking to a . . . um . . . civil servant. They found her car in a parking lot where they'd set a ruse. You understand?"

"A trap, not a ruse," I said distractedly.

"Right. A while ago the girl came to pick up the car. She was arrested. Put in prison. You can go, Tarpon."

I nodded. I walked toward the door. I thought of all the shit that was going to hit the fan. But I was more concerned with something else. I raised my head when I got to the door.

"If she's in jail," I said, "you won't be able to look her in the whites of her eyes. You'll have to let justice run its course." He didn't answer; he was almost smiling. "Whaddya say about that?" I added.

"If she's the one who killed my little girl, I'll destroy her. Wherever she is. Even in prison."

"Fine," I said. "See ya, Gorizia."

"Farewell, Tarpon."

I walked through the door. In the vestibule, Caruso and the Mercedes driver were playing Chinese checkers on a side table. They gave me back my watch, my keys, my pen. Then I left.

There were two parking tickets on the windshield of the Aronde. This time, I bothered to tear them up and throw them in the gutter. I got in the car. I was tired and hungry. I thought it would be better to go home and wait for the cops to come sooner or later.

It was 1:15 p.m. when I parked the Aronde on rue Saint-Martin. I found a grocery shop and bought a can of William Saurin cassoulet and a bottle of Amstel.

As I was climbing my stairs, I almost knocked over a small wrinkled man wearing a brown three-piece suit who pulled off the feat of being bald *and* having dandruff.

"You wouldn't be Mr. Eugène Louis Marie Tarpon?" he asked as if he were very busy.

"I am."

"I have a summons for you."

He fought with the clasp on his briefcase. In the end, he gave me a piece of paper and made me sign a receipt.

"Have a good day," he practically shouted as he went on his way.

The summons summoned me to appear before Justice Desrousseaux on Friday (the next day) at three in the afternoon. I folded the paper as carefully as I could with my hands full of cassoulet and beer and stuffed it in my pocket. I finished climbing my stairs and went into my place.

The place was in a bit of disorder. Not the kind left by a burglar. The kind left by an illegal searcher. From what I could tell, the police had strolled around my place after I was kidnapped.

I put my cassoulet and beer in the kitchen. I got undressed and started washing at the kitchen sink. Immediately the phone began to ring.

"I've tried to call you half a dozen times," said Haymann. "I started thinking I should send the cops to the Hilton. Where have you been? Why didn't you call me?"

I briefly explained everything to him. My hand was full of soap and it was getting all over the phone.

"Gorizia?" Haymann repeated. "Don't know the guy. But I have to admit I'm not all that familiar with today's underworld. Say, I'm right by the hotel now. Do you know?"

"What hotel? What are you talking about?"

"Stop playing the fool, Tarpon! The hotel where you were staying with Memphis Charles. Under the name Mr. and Mrs. Malone. There's news. Bad news. Sad news."

"Make me sad."

"Under the mattress," said Haymann. "They found a bunch of dirty photos. Pictures of Miss Griselda with various partners. And a list with the names of all of them. I couldn't find out anything about the names. But in any case, it was good blackmail material. And that's not the saddest thing."

"So make me sadder."

"The handle of a knife. Know anything about that? And a rather bloody one. Alfonsino was also killed with a knife, wasn't he?"

"Yes," I sighed. "And a broken knife too. The handle was missing."

"I have the feeling it's been found."

We didn't speak for a good twenty seconds. I heard both of us breathing on the line.

"Did you think the kid was nice?" Haymann finally asked.

"Yes," I said. "Yes, I thought she was nice."

I'd scarcely finished our conversation and had just put my bare foot in the sink when the phone rang again. This time it was Gérard Sergent. He wanted to know if there was any news, what I was doing, what I had done. I told him where things stood. I didn't mention Gorizia, the crying man, because I didn't want to destroy the picture a man has of his mother. I told him almost everything else, including my travels with Memphis Charles. In any case, he would have found out sooner or later.

He took it much better than I'd feared.

"You thought you were doing the right thing," he said.

"Yes."

"And what do you think now, Tarpon?"

I asked myself the same question.

"I'm not sure that the kid is guilty," said Sergent.

"Why?"

"Those things that were hidden...under the mattress, you said? That seems like a ridiculous hiding place. Especially in a hotel."

"I agree," I said.

My God, that cowhand was cheering me up.

"Stay on it, will you?" he asked.

"Yes."

"And besides," he said, "a girl, a young girl, huh? Killing people is not a job for a young girl."

Another guy who thought that woman is gentle, woman is fragile, woman is pure. Nonetheless, he was cheering me up.

We chatted a little longer. Then I went back to washing up.

This time, I managed to work without being disturbed. I scrubbed from head to toe and shaved. I put on a pair of old corduroy trousers, a checked shirt, and black nylon socks. I put on my slippers. I opened the can of cassoulet, poured the contents in a pot and heated them up. I sat down at the table with the beer and the cassoulet. I ate straight out of the pot and drank straight from the bottle. While I was eating, I thought.

When I'd finished eating, it was two fifty on Thursday afternoon; all this fucking mess had started Monday evening, and I'd aged ten years in two and a half days. I walked to the phone, picked it up, and dialed Thunder Films.

Lyssenko had just got in and they passed the phone to him without too much fuss.

"The dough they wanted in exchange for the dirty photograph," I said. "You were supposed to put it at Montparnasse station today at five p.m., right?"

"I'm sure I told you that I haven't the slightest intention of..."

"I know," I interrupted. "But would you mind doing what they asked with a briefcase full of old newspapers or something like that?"

He thought for a moment.

"Are you setting a trap?"

"Well, yeah."

He grumbled.

"The dimwit is probably setting us a trap too," he said. "You'd have to be mentally retarded to want to extort money like that, wouldn't you? I mean, really. The lockers at Montparnasse? I smell a rat."

"Obviously," I said. "You'll be attacked on the way there."

"What?"

He was shouting, but out of excitement rather than panic.

"The guy told you to be at Montparnasse at a specific time," I explained patiently. "But he said to leave your office with the dough at a certain time too. At four, right? He's going to look out for you, follow you, and take the cash from you on the way. It's obvious."

Lyssenko was quiet for a moment. Then he said, "Holy shit! You should be a screenwriter!"

"Nevertheless," I said, "will you do what I said?"

"Good Lord!" Lyssenko shouted enthusiastically. "You'll come with me, right? You'll hide near the office, you'll follow me, and when he tries to take the briefcase, the two of us will overpower him, right? Right? That's what you're saying? Good Lord, I'm gonna make a movie out of this! You think the blackmailer and the kid's murderer are one and the same guy?"

I said I had no idea. Which didn't put a damper on his enthusiasm.

"We'll figure it out," he said somewhat obscurely. "What time can you be here, Tarpon?"

"With all the traffic, I doubt I'll make it before four. I won't go into the office. I'll be hiding somewhere on the street when you come out."

His excitement was palpable. He patiently explained what he'd be wearing, and the make and color of his car. Before he hung up, he told me to make tracks.

I hung up as well and stared at the phone. I should have called Coquelet. I didn't.

I paced around the apartment, trying to remember what I'd done with my spiffy Hi-Power, where I could have stowed it the day before yesterday before I was jumped by the pro-Palestinians. I finally found the thing in a dresser drawer after having searched in much less plausible places. The firearms permit was resting on top of it, with a cigarette burn on the paper. Clearly the police had been there. I checked that the gun was loaded. I wasn't thinking about using it on the street. I even had my doubts that anyone was going to attack Lyssenko at that point. But you never know, and I'd brandish my weapon with more conviction if it were loaded.

I crammed the Belgian-German-Polish Browning in the side pocket of a corduroy jacket that matched my trousers. I pulled on the jacket, put my shoes back on, and walked toward the door. When a drop of blood fell on my hand, it was exactly 3:15 in the afternoon.

22

AT FIRST I thought it was water. My building was very old and rent-controlled, and the owner did as little as possible as far as upkeep was concerned. So nothing is exactly watertight in this fucked-up piece of real estate, neither the pipes nor the walls, and I thought there must have been a leak at Stanislavski's place, dripping down through his floor. Then I looked at my hand and noticed that the drop was pinkish. I raised my eyes and saw a large brown stain on the ceiling.

I left my apartment and climbed up a flight. Stanislavski didn't answer when I rang and knocked. It was only then that my mind fully grasped the idea that it was blood dripping down from the tailor's. So I broke down the door with a strong kick just below the lock. The plaster exploded and the door slammed open against the wall. I went in.

Inside: absolute carnage. The valiant little tailor had defended himself for a long time. The furniture was all overturned. The sewing machine was smashed to bits. All along a bedroom wall, the cretonne drapes had been torn down. The floor-to-ceiling shelves behind them had been swept clean and wrecked, books strewn everywhere. Stanislavski must have clung to those shelves while he was being murdered and flung everything to the floor.

The valiant little tailor was now curled up between the

bed and the wall. His body was partly covered by the cretonne drapes, and partly by books. He'd been stabbed in the back multiple times, maybe ten or fifteen. He looked like mincemeat. He'd been drained of all his blood. I touched him cautiously. I couldn't believe he was really dead. And I couldn't fathom why he'd been killed.

The blood wasn't fresh. It had coagulated. It must have been the last drop that'd made its way through his soaked floor to fall on my hand. Stanislavski had been dead for at least an hour. Probably more. He was already completely rigid. When I touched him, I noticed he was curled up on a book that was half torn to shreds and completely soaked in blood. I took the book out from under him, along with a handful of torn-out pages gripped in his fist. Dried blood doesn't look at all like blood. The book and its torn-out pages seemed to have been dipped in coffee. They formed a sticky brown bundle. It was revolting.

At first glance, it didn't seem like the weapon was still on the scene. I surveyed the two rooms looking for I don't know what; a clue, I suppose. My hands began to tremble violently and then my teeth started to chatter. Saliva dripped between my chattering teeth onto my chin. My ears burned and my vision was blurry. I swore several times under my breath, tapping softly on the fallen furniture with my knuckles.

I set the blood-soaked book down on the telephone shelf. The title of the book was *The Mass Psychology of Fascism*. I laughed nervously. I left the tailor's apartment and went down the stairs. Between the fourth and third floor, I noticed I was still holding the torn-out pages. I stuffed them in my pocket. I continued down the stairs and my teeth continued chattering. Stanislavski and his tea. The way he said my name. Stanislavski, the gentle tailor. Oh, God!

On the last flight of stairs, I bumped into the lady drunk who serves as the concierge.

"You don't look so hot," she remarked.

"Mr. Stanislavski died in his bedroom," I said.

Her mouth formed a shocked *o*. Before she could react in another way, I left the building and headed for rue Saint-Martin.

I got into Haymann's Aronde. I took off. I drove fast. I went toward Saint-Lazare. An insect was gnawing away at the insides of my head.

Near the train station, I got stuck in a traffic jam. I looked at my watch. Ten to four. I stuck a hand in my pocket and pulled out the bits of filthy paper that Stanislavski had clung to with such force as he died. Through the stains and splatters, I could make out a rather obscure text:

"...Judaizing of our spiritual life and mammonizing of our natural instinct for procreation will sooner or...[bits were missing]...osterity. The sin against blood and race is..."

It seemed it was a quote from Hitler. The traffic jam moved along with me. I passed the train station and turned toward the north. Five or six minutes later I stopped near a crosswalk at the entrance of the small steep road where Thunder Films was housed. From there I could see the exit of the building where the office was. It was three minutes to four. I looked again at the paper in my hand:

We understand by "vices of the parents" their habi...
ix with the blood of another race, and also p...ith the
blood of a Jew, thus making pure blood...tamination
by the "worldwide Jewish plague." We...socialist-anti-
Semitis...belongs to the irrational...domain of

syphilitic phobia. According...thus attempt using all means to reach purity of...to the purity of blood.

It took me a moment to understand. But then I realized who was waiting for Lyssenko somewhere in one of the parked cars or else in the little café across from Thunder Films. And just then, Lyssenko came out of the building, early by a minute and a half. And Gérard Sergent came out of a little café.

I tore out of the Aronde like a madman and raced onto the street screaming as I tried to pull out the Hi-Power. The sight got stuck in a hole in my lining. I ripped it all out, lining and gun. Gérard Sergent started to run too. He was crossing the street. On the opposite sidewalk, Lyssenko had turned toward me as I was screaming, and he seemed completely dumbstruck. Gérard Sergent was about to catch up to him. I stood still, legs slightly apart and feet forming a forty-five-degree angle; I cocked my good old gun and extended my arm almost all the way at about eye level, like we'd been taught. I pulled the trigger. The bang deafened me. Sergent fell on all fours in the gutter at Lyssenko's feet. I didn't know where I'd hit him. I saw him start to get up. He took a carving knife out of his houndstooth jacket. Lyssenko threw his briefcase at Sergent's head and fled into the building as fast as his legs could carry him.

It's over, I thought, as I trotted toward the wounded man. He'd finished standing up and turned toward me. The entire right side of his face was covered in blood. I'd had just about enough blood for one day.

"Pig, son of a drunkard, son of a whore," he said as he walked to meet me.

I aimed my automatic at his heart.

"Drop the knife, old man," I said.

He threw himself at me and I pulled the trigger, shouting in disgust. The Hi-Power jammed. I found out later that the first cartridge hadn't ejected. Rust. Sergent ran at me again and bounced off me. He fell backward and I fell to my knees. He sniggered. I saw the handle of the carving knife sticking out between my ribs, and I felt the steel inside my body.

"Filthy Jew," said Gérard Sergent, which was ridiculous: I'm from the Allier region in central France.

Then we both passed out, and after a while the emergency services picked us up.

23

"I'D SAY he's more of a sicko than anything else," I told Haymann.

The journalist was sitting at my bedside, on a metal chair with peeling ivory paint, and the smell of his raincoat mingled with the smell of the hospital room. He nodded and took out a Gitane Maïs cigarette.

"There's no smoking in here," I reminded him.

"Fuck them."

Haymann lit his cigarette. He pulled on it several times in a row, voluptuously. His cigarette was drenched in saliva.

"Sick in the head is no excuse," he said.

"Try to understand. Imagine. Imagine his childhood. Three years younger than his sister. And his mother... My God, Marius Gorizia said to me the other day, that Madam Sergent was a fucking whore. Just think about it. In a tiny village in the country. The local trollop. One guy after another. Traveling salesmen, ranchers, deputy mayors, soldiers. Just picture the father who hangs himself. Not without first having drunk himself blind on plonk and Calvados."

"Ah, the joys of the countryside," Haymann snickered. "I know. I've been there. Makes local and national news. The hereditary alcoholic who massacres his family with a pitchfork. That wasn't the impression Sergent gave me."

I shrugged, very unobtrusively because I wasn't allowed

to move. I had been sewn up only forty-eight hours ago. The blade hadn't managed to puncture my vital organs, but still, it had cut a fifteen-centimeter passageway through my flesh. It was sheer chance it hadn't come out my back. According to the emergency room docs, I'd been amazingly lucky.

"Gérard Sergent," I said, "had it rough. Drunkard for a father. Whore for a mother. Father committed suicide. Sister Louise, who started sleeping around just when he hit puberty. We should have understood when he kept repeating that she was pure, not slutty, that she'd never fucked anyone. Jesus, we should have understood. Just think about it. Gérard and Louise sleeping in the same room. When Louise comes home at dawn, Gérard spies on her through his eyelashes when she gets undressed. She smells of man, another man ..."

"Enough with the fairy tales," Haymann interjected.

"... and he can't have her," I continued, as if I were dreaming. "Everyone possesses her, except him. Just like everyone, except him, possessed his mother. And that goes on for years. Louise goes away with those 'gentlemen' from the big city. She makes filthy movies. Gérard comes to see her every now and then. He knows she lives in the gutter. She lets Jews and wops fuck her. When exactly did Gérard develop his ideas about Jews and wops? We can only guess."

"He didn't lack for opportunities," Haymann snarled. "No one does."

"As far as when he did it," I sighed, "I don't know the details. I haven't had much time to think about the details. I'm full of drugs. I keep falling asleep."

Haymann cracked his knuckles. The cracks echoed in my skull. It was annoying.

"Monday night," said the journalist, "Gérard went to see his sister. He'd been there for an hour; they checked. He'd wanted to screw Louise for ten years. That night, he went at it. We'll never know why. We'd have to get inside his head. In any case, he went at it. She resisted. He didn't manage to possess her completely because all of a sudden he was impotent. He killed her. It's as simple as that."

"Simple..." I repeated.

"He used Memphis Charles's knife. As soon as he calms down, he tries to be clever. He calls the cops. He imitates a woman's voice to say that two girls are fighting on the ground floor of the villa. Then he hangs up."

Haymann took a drag on his cigarette. Some underlings had entered from the rear of the ward with rolling carts. Food. Even though my intestines hadn't been perforated, my insides were a bit upset—a sort of postoperative shock—and all I got was rice.

"He spent the rest of the night wandering around," Haymann continued. "In the morning, he took a room at a hotel as if he'd just arrived on the first train. And then he went to his sister's. He pretended he'd just learned about the murder. He went to the cops, who took him to the morgue to have him identify her. That's when I grabbed him to bring him to you. I don't know why he accepted. Maybe country boys read too many detective novels. Maybe he enjoyed playing with fire."

"Playing with death," I said. "With punishment."

"Stop imagining fucking Freudian psychology everywhere," Haymann said. "Just because you've seen the light in some book on psychoanalysis, it doesn't mean you have to become obsessed with it."

"It's time, ladies and gentlemen," the head of the ward said for the third time, tapping against the glass of her private little office with a metal object, a spoon I think.

"We can also imagine that Gérard Sergent wanted to stay informed about the progress of the investigation," said Haymann. "Or else I don't know what."

The head of the ward came toward us. The other visitors had left. Haymann relit his cigarette that had gone out.

"Evil is never black and white," he declared pedantically through the butt of his cigarette.

"You've got to leave, sir. It's time," said the head of the ward.

"Can't you see I'm speaking!"

"Come now, sir. On your way."

"The other murders," said Haymann, "I just can't understand. He really was out of his mind."

"You must leave now, sir!" said the head of the ward with a trace of exasperation in her voice.

She was flushed with irritation. She was horribly ugly. Haymann stood up. He took a paperback out of his raincoat pocket. He placed it on my bedside table, banging it against the metal. It was *Three Essays on the Theory of Sexuality*.

"In spite of its title, there's not much tits and ass in it," declared the journalist. "But I thought it would put you to sleep. I'll come back this evening and you'll give me the psychoanalytic reasons for the other murders."

Then he left, cackling.

24

Excerpts from the weekly magazine Detection *the following Thursday. Article entitled* THE INSANE FRATRICIDE WHO WANTED TO CASTRATE ALL THE MEN WHO'D OBTAINED "FAVORS" FROM HIS SISTER.

———

... It was the sight of blood on the body half-undressed by the final convulsions of death that triggered something evil in the obsessed brain of the murderer. He seemed to believe he had to strike again, kill again, until he was caught or there was no one else to strike. Scholars and doctors are aware of this guilt complex phenomenon. From that point on, Gérard Sergent became a deadly maniac, a pathetic archangel brandishing his knife like a steel penis, frantically inflicting what he so wanted someone to inflict on him.

ERASE THE FILTH

The fratricide's sick mind turned almost automatically toward those who'd soiled his sister and Gérard then began with all his might to wash this filth away in blood. He first attacked Edouard Alfonsino, the handsome but unsavory lad who managed to enthrall the starlet and make her his slave during the mad orgies he organized in the ritzy neighborhoods for shady groups where fine-looking young men, restless artists, gigolos, movie producers hungry for new flesh, and other representatives of a shifty "dolce vita" rubbed shoulders in wisps of marijuana smoke and vapors of alcohol.

In addition, from some of his sister's lapses, Gérard learned that all sorts of files with quantities of compromising photographs could be found at Handsome Eddy's. These photos are now in the hands of Commissioner Coquelet, causing many to fear for their reputations. The killer made his decision. Handsome Eddy would be his next victim.

On the morning of Wednesday, April 18, as soon as he entered the home of the organizer of these sex parties, Sergent struck. One blow was all it took. During Eddy's final spasms, the blade broke. The murderer, with stunning insensitivity, took the time to rummage through the studio of his victim lying on the carpet and stole the compromising documents he'd come to get. Only once he'd found them did he flee, the bloody knife handle in his pocket, clutching Eddy's files against him.

A DEMENTED SCHEME:
ALL-OUT SLAUGHTER

Even before the assassin became aware of the scandalous photos, he'd outlined in his clouded brain a demented scheme of slaughter. Less than an hour after handsome Eddy's death, pneumatics flew all over Paris, addressed to several representatives of that shady milieu to which the "touching" Griselda belonged. Each envelope contained a photograph and a message from the madman demanding the next day, at different hours of the afternoon and evening, the sum of one million old francs. The various recipients all had one thing in common: all of them, at one time or another, had been blessed with the favors of a starlet hungry for pleasure. The photos show these men in the arms of the young woman in a breathtaking series of lascivious, diabolical positions of paroxysmal vice. These photos are now with the police, who are keeping them away from the sight of the morbidly curious.

As he would confess to Commissioner Coquelet and Officer Coccioli, the criminal did not simply intend to blackmail his victims. He was possessed by the desire to kill them. Only death and horrible, ritual mutilations seemed a fair way to make these men who were ostensibly "good fathers" atone for how they had secretly made Griselda the object of their unimaginable derangement. Each would get his due, and this is how the obsessed man proposed to massacre more than six people with bestial cruelty.

… But fate had put in Sergent's path an unexpected victim who would lead to his downfall.

MORE THAN TWENTY STAB WOUNDS

That victim was Thaddée Stanislavski, a gentle sixty-five-year-old tailor who lived upstairs from the detective Eugène Tarpon. The discreet little artisan liked to help out his neighbors. He'd promised the former gendarme he'd call Charlotte

Schultz, alias Memphis Charles, in the small hotel where she was hiding out, to advise her to go to the police.

It was then that fate struck. Just when the tailor was about to call, his doorbell rang. It was Sergent. With portentous recklessness, the murderer had come to see Tarpon to ask if there was any news about his sister.

The tailor was guileless. And trusting. He knew Sergent, whom he'd already seen with Tarpon. It never occurred to him that the fat blond boy with his naive eyes could be his own sister's monstrous killer and was thinking about committing more murders.

Stanislavski invited the young man in and even, as the investigation would later prove, offered him tea. Unaware of the subtleties of a criminal investigation, he thought he could call Charlotte Schultz while Sergent was in the next room listening to the conversation.

When the conversation ended, a demoniacal plan had hatched in the tortured mind of the assassin. He demanded to know the number that Stanislavski called. Did the tailor obey, unsuspecting? Or did he refuse? Did Sergent strike him to destroy a bothersome witness, or was that same unbelievable ferocity he'd demonstrated earlier, stabbing the tailor more than twenty times, a kind of torture that the madman inflicted on his victim to make him talk? We'll never know.

Nonetheless, the old man died in a pool of blood. It didn't take long for Sergent, who finally got his hands on the precious telephone number, to identify the hotel where Charlotte Schultz was hiding out. The frightened young woman had just abandoned her hotel room. Sergent went into the room and planted the incriminating evidence that he hoped would implicate the stuntwoman, giving him time to flee with the millions he hoped to collect that very evening. But he hadn't counted on Eugène Tarpon's dazzling intuition.

———

The article went on and on. It was illustrated with six photos, two of Griselda Zapata in lascivious poses, one of Memphis Charles leaving Judge Desrousseaux's chambers, an old one of Gérard Sergent after his meeting with the draft board, another of Commissioner Coquelet and Officer Coccioli, and the last one of investigator Eugène Tarpon (he of the dazzling intuition), shown here in his gendarme's uniform.

25

I ONLY stayed in the hospital a week because I didn't have much money on the horizon. I went back to my apartment where I had to spend another two weeks in bed waiting to heal. I learned that the check for 3,500 francs that Sergent had given to me would have bounced anyway, so I wouldn't have been any better off even if I'd had the time to cash it before things went south.

Haymann was an angel. He came to see me every day and he paid my concierge to bring me up food and other stuff. She was usually drunk and would tell me stories about her family. It was restful.

Best of all, Haymann managed to get me 2,000 new francs in exchange for the exclusive rights to my story, and he concocted an astonishingly flamboyant account of the whole affair that was published in the papers and even translated for an Italian weekly. He got some good publicity for me so that Coquelet and Coccioli wouldn't bug me too much. I saw Judge Desrousseaux when I was finally up and about. He scolded me, you could say, but I wasn't indicted for anything.

And then, a week after I got out of the hospital, I got a check for a million old francs from a guy named Terracini. I never knew who that guy was, but you don't have to be a genius to figure out it came from Marius Gorizia.

So, once the hospital and other things, including my debt, were paid off, I found myself with a million, which is a bit unusual for someone who'd gotten a knife stuck in his gut.

Life was, in a way, beautiful.

When I felt better, I tried to go see Alain Lhuillier, the young guy who'd come to me that first night because he was being pressured, and whom I'd almost punched when I was drunk. I wanted to tell him not to despair, that I'd be happy to take care of his business and that, basically, there was still a way to muddle through this fucking universe.

It was nearly impossible to find him because he hadn't left me his address. And when at last I managed to locate his "nightclub," I was told he'd stepped down, run off to the mountains, no one knew where he was or what had become of him. The big guns had taken over. I was sorry. I felt I was at fault.

Memphis Charles came to see me. She too had gotten off without a hitch. She was still well dressed, and very pretty. I hadn't heard from her for a month because of some love story, as I understood it. She told me she'd married a sound engineer. I congratulated her. I never saw her again.

That's about it.

No, I forgot. I don't know whether Gorizia had something to do with it or it was remorse or madness or something else, but while he was remanded in custody, Gérard Sergent managed to kill himself with a nail.

AFTERWORD

> They were nearly all Islanders in the Pequod, *Isolatoes*
> too, I call such, not acknowledging the common con-
> tinent of men, but each *Isolato* living on a separate
> continent of his own.
>   —Herman Melville, *Moby-Dick*

HERMAN MELVILLE called them "isolatoes"—the word
he coined for those among us who don't have much truck
with fellow humans. The bonds of society, except in odd and
extenuating circumstances, are not really for them. Love,
marriage, family seem as strange, distant institutions, things
one might observe with a notebook in the other hand. At
best, there are a couple of old comrades accumulated on life's
journey to whom one might turn when things go south. For
isolatoes, the most constant of companions are those voices
inside the head.

Jean-Patrick Manchette's protagonists are isolatoes. Georges
Gerfault in *Three to Kill*, Julie Ballanger in *The Mad and the
Bad*, Martin Terrier in *The Prone Gunman*, Aimée Joubert
in *Fatale*: windowless monads, all of them. Memorable, violent, alone.

Eugène Tarpon, Manchette's private eye here, is among
these nations of one. Like many fictional private eyes he's
come to the end of his rope; in fact, as the novel begins, he's

already thrown his badge in the river. Only an unlikely client—is there any other kind?—coming through the door puts his retirement plans on ice.

You perhaps know (and Manchette certainly knew) Dashiell Hammett's Flitcraft story, an existential parable embedded within *The Maltese Falcon*. It contains the sentence, "He adjusted himself to beams falling, and then no more of them fell, and he adjusted himself to them not falling." In *No Room at the Morgue* it goes the other way: As we meet him, Tarpon has submitted to a certain quiescence. He has adjusted himself to a life where beams no longer fall. And then one does. Providing him with a headache, us with a narrative.

As is so often the case with Manchette, the shadow of May '68 hovers over all, much as the shadow of the Occupation hovers over the novels of Patrick Modiano. It's what our Lacanian friends would call "the structuring absence." The France of Eugène Tarpon is littered with the debris of failed revolt. If those who make half a revolution only dig their own graves, Tarpon's journey is a slow stumble across that graveyard: his Paris is a Père Lachaise of the soul.

Yet Tarpon is no soixante-huitard; rather, he's a retired (or cashiered) gendarme who killed a militant during a protest.* When we meet him in the "fifth floor, no elevator" flat near Les Halles that serves as his home, his office, his life, he's drinking pastis straight, his bank account has cratered, he's within twenty-four hours of going home to mom in the provinces. The adventure/misadventure into which

---

*Imagine a Sam Spade who, like Hammett, had previously worked as a Pinkerton but, unlike Hammett, had also been a strikebreaker.

he is then swirled—with about the same degree of agency here as Dorothy when a twister swept her to Oz—takes him to that most Manchettian of locales, an abandoned house in the country, where pro-Palestinian firebrands and American mobsters clash by night. Tarpon's attitude toward the former mirrors Manchette's own—as he wrote in his diary, "the collapse of leftism into terrorism is the collapse of the revolution into spectacle."

From the carnage of the countryside, Tarpon makes his bloodied way back to Paris—to what might nominally be called civilization—only to be followed, abducted, drugged, shot at, and stabbed by a farrago of gangsters, pornographers, miscreants, sociopaths, and killers. In this upside-down world, the nice guys turn out to be the cops. They don't beat you up unless there's a reason for them to do so.

For all of the gimlet-eyed precision with which Manchette observes human activity in the post-'68 landscape, he always gives us a character or two who behave well, and with empathy for their fellow beings. In *Three to Kill* it was Raguse, the kindly alpine recluse who takes in our protagonist. Here it's the journalist Haymann, who helps Tarpon when he doesn't really have to; and the upstairs neighbor, the elderly tailor Stanislavski, who has never harmed a soul, and suffers the consequences. Manchette uses these figures to cast in high relief the bad faith and worse behavior of the rest of us, caught in the convulsions of late, or one may say after-hours, capitalism.

The language he uses to depict these convulsions only heightens the terror and the absurdity—André Breton would surely recognize in Manchette a fellow practitioner of *humour noire*. As Tarpon narrates, "I was making up theories in my head: Was Haymann an Israeli agent? And was it in fact

Memphis Charles they'd tried to assassinate the other night? My theories were collapsing one by one, but I started constructing them all over again. At the same time, I was dreaming of steak frites. And it was getting mixed up in my theories. Béarnaise sauce was dripping down the faces of Palestinians. In my head, I mean. In my head." Or, more offhandedly: "Memphis Charles had dragged the American who was still alive into the workshop and she was attaching him to the pipes. Life goes on, like the song says."

Still, from time to time—and this is what makes *No Room at the Morgue* so poignant—we're also allowed a window into the heart, an access given legitimacy by the fact that it occurs so rarely and against a landscape so invariably gray. Here we have a mobster who inexplicably breaks down in tears. We don't understand it but are moved. And then, later, we do understand it and are moved yet more deeply. For Manchette, these moments of fragility, of tenderness, aren't moments of weakness. But they're not moments of strength, either.

No Room at the Morgue and its sequel, *Que d'os!*, are the only two of Manchette's novels to feature a private eye as protagonist. Though in Manchette there's never a shortage of killers for hire, killers for the hell of it, casual psychotics, mercenaries, and the corruption of each and every institution, there are relatively few police in his policiers, and very little mystery about the who in whodunit. The Tarpon novels are in some sense a throwback to a time when the genre was more tightly defined, its tropes less problematic. We've got a down-at-heels P.I. here, and bad guys, and a femme-more-or-less-fatale, and a couple of cops either of whom could be played by Lino Ventura. But Manchette certainly isn't slumming, or doing a genre turn to please his fans. As Manchette asks, "What do you do when you re-do [the classic American crime novels] at a distance—distant because the moment of that something is long gone? The American-style *polar* had its day. Writing in 1970 meant taking a new social reality into account, but it also meant acknowledging that the *polar*-form was finished because its time was finished: re-employing an obsolete form implies employing it referentially, honoring it by criticizing it, exaggerating it, distorting it from top to bottom."* Or as he put it more bluntly (and more flamboyantly): "The avenues opened by the '*néo-polar*' were gradually conquered either by *littérateurs* (Artists with a capital A) or else by Stalino-Trotskyite Gorbachevophiles."†

No Room at the Morgue is, then, a story that begins with Marx and ends in Freud, stopping along the way at Wilhelm Reich. In some sense the novel is an omnium-gatherum, a cabinet of wonders containing all of Manchette's favored objects: a broke, alienated protagonist with a great future behind him; men at the very end of their tether; women in dissociation and distress; a supporting cast of radicals, terrorists, antiterrorists, libertines, mobsters—isolatoes all!—whose mental state could at best be called fragile. All of them driving around the high-numbered arrondissements in beater

---

*Interview with Manchette, *Polar 12* (1980); reprinted in Manchette, *Chroniques* (Paris: Editions Payot & Rivages, 1996), 16, retrieved and translated by Donald Nicholson-Smith.

†"La position du romancier noir solitaire," interview by Yannick Bourg, *Combo!* 8 (1991).

Peugeots and Simcas that, like their drivers, could at any moment be taking their last breaths.

In Preston Sturges's sublime *The Palm Beach Story*, Tom Jeffers (Joel McCrea) is tracking his wife (Claudette Colbert), who's decamped to Florida. Jeffers follows. He finds a sleeping-car porter who was working the train that brought his wife to Palm Beach. Jeffers asks of the porter, "Was she alone?" The porter responds, "Well, you might practically say she's alone. The gentleman who got off with her gave me ten cents from New York to Jacksonville: she's alone, but she don't know it."

So many of Manchette's protagonists are exactly that: They're alone, but they don't know it. Or at least don't know it until the events of the narrative hammer home, with impeccable vengeance, that bleak and final truth. But here, Eugène Tarpon is alone, knows it, makes no bones about it. He doesn't see solitude as something to be remedied—rather, it's a given, like the beer he drinks, the cassoulet he eats right out of the can, the cherished, rusted Browning that jams at the instant of need.

—HOWARD A. RODMAN

TITLES IN SERIES

For a complete list of titles, visit www.nyrb.com or write to:
Catalog Requests, NYRB, 435 Hudson Street, New York, NY 10014

J.R. ACKERLEY Hindoo Holiday
J.R. ACKERLEY My Dog Tulip
J.R. ACKERLEY My Father and Myself
J.R. ACKERLEY We Think the World of You
HENRY ADAMS The Jeffersonian Transformation
RENATA ADLER Pitch Dark
RENATA ADLER Speedboat
AESCHYLUS Prometheus Bound; translated by Joel Agee
ROBERT AICKMAN Compulsory Games
LEOPOLDO ALAS His Only Son *with* Doña Berta
CÉLESTE ALBARET Monsieur Proust
DANTE ALIGHIERI The Inferno
KINGSLEY AMIS The Alteration
KINGSLEY AMIS Dear Illusion: Collected Stories
KINGSLEY AMIS Ending Up
KINGSLEY AMIS Girl, 20
KINGSLEY AMIS The Green Man
KINGSLEY AMIS Lucky Jim
KINGSLEY AMIS The Old Devils
KINGSLEY AMIS One Fat Englishman
KINGSLEY AMIS Take a Girl Like You
ROBERTO ARLT The Seven Madmen
U.R. ANANTHAMURTHY Samskara: A Rite for a Dead Man
IVO ANDRIĆ Omer Pasha Latas
WILLIAM ATTAWAY Blood on the Forge
W.H. AUDEN (EDITOR) The Living Thoughts of Kierkegaard
W.H. AUDEN W. H. Auden's Book of Light Verse
ERICH AUERBACH Dante: Poet of the Secular World
EVE BABITZ Eve's Hollywood
EVE BABITZ I Used to Be Charming: The Rest of Eve Babitz
EVE BABITZ Slow Days, Fast Company: The World, the Flesh, and L.A.
DOROTHY BAKER Cassandra at the Wedding
DOROTHY BAKER Young Man with a Horn
J.A. BAKER The Peregrine
S. JOSEPHINE BAKER Fighting for Life
HONORÉ DE BALZAC The Human Comedy: Selected Stories
HONORÉ DE BALZAC The Memoirs of Two Young Wives
HONORÉ DE BALZAC The Unknown Masterpiece *and* Gambara
VICKI BAUM Grand Hotel
SYBILLE BEDFORD A Favorite of the Gods *and* A Compass Error
SYBILLE BEDFORD Jigsaw
SYBILLE BEDFORD A Legacy
SYBILLE BEDFORD A Visit to Don Otavio: A Mexican Journey
MAX BEERBOHM The Prince of Minor Writers: The Selected Essays of Max Beerbohm
MAX BEERBOHM Seven Men
STEPHEN BENATAR Wish Her Safe at Home
FRANS G. BENGTSSON The Long Ships
WALTER BENJAMIN The Storyteller Essays
ALEXANDER BERKMAN Prison Memoirs of an Anarchist
GEORGES BERNANOS Mouchette